Here's what teens are saying about Bluford High:

"As soon as I finished one book, I couldn't wait to start the next one. No books have ever made me do that before."
—*Terrance W.*

"The suspense got to be so great I could feel the blood pounding in my ears."
—*Yolanda E.*

"Once I started reading them, I just couldn't stop, not even to go to sleep."
—*Brian M.*

"Great books! I hope they write more."
—*Eric J.*

"When I finished these books, I went back to the beginning and read them all over again. That's how much I loved them."
—*Caren B.*

"I found it very easy to lose myself in these books. They kept my interest from beginning to end and were always realistic. The characters are vivid, and the endings left me in eager anticipation of the next book."
—*Keziah J.*

BLUFORD HIGH

Lost and Found

A Matter of Trust

Secrets in the Shadows

Someone to Love Me

The Bully

Payback

Until We Meet Again

Blood Is Thicker

Brothers in Arms

Summer of Secrets

The Bully

PAUL LANGAN

Series Editor: Paul Langan

SCHOLASTIC INC.
New York Toronto London Auckland Sydney
Mexico City New Delhi Hong Kong Buenos Aires

ISBN-13: 978-0-545-03546-0
ISBN-10: 0-545-03546-5

Copyright © 2002 by Townsend Press, Inc.
Discussion questions adapted from
Teacher's Guide to The Bluford Series by Eliza A. Comodromos,
copyright © 2004 by Townsend Press.
Other teacher's edition material copyright © 2007 by Scholastic Inc.
All rights reserved. Published by Scholastic Inc.,
557 Broadway, New York, NY 10012, by arrangement
with Townsend Press, Inc. SCHOLASTIC and associated logos
are trademarks and/or registered trademarks of Scholastic Inc.

12 11 10 9 8 7 6 5 4 3 2 1   7 8 9 10 11 12/0

Printed in the U.S.A.   01

This teacher's edition first printing, August 2007

Chapter 1

With a cold November wind stabbing through his jacket, Darrell Mercer took one last walk with his best friend, Malik Stone.

"Man, I can't believe you're movin' to California tomorrow," Malik said. "I just can't believe I won't see you no more."

Darrell shook his head. He could not believe it either. In just a few hours, he would leave the only neighborhood he had ever known in his fifteen years. Soon his street, his school, and every friend he had in the world would be thousands of miles away. Thinking about what was ahead of him, Darrell felt like a man going to his own hanging.

"I'll miss you, man," Darrell said, his voice wavering.

The boys had known each other since first grade at Harrison School on 44th

Street. Their neighborhood was definitely not one of Philadelphia's best. Most of the buildings were old and decaying, and graffiti covered just about every one. Some houses were vacant, and a few had broken windows. Abandoned cars rusted along many streets, and occasionally local newscasts would run a story about city crime and feature this area as an example. To many people, the neighborhood was trouble, but to Darrell and his friends, it was home. True, there were guys selling drugs on street corners. But there were also good kids like Malik, Big Reggie, and Mark. Because of them, Darrell had never felt alone.

Inside the rundown homes that lined Darrell's block, there were always people to turn to in times of trouble. Across the street was old Mr. Corbitt, who sat on his porch each day and waved at everyone who passed by. And in the corner house was Mrs. Morton. She made sweet-potato pie for people in the neighborhood, especially Darrell and his mother.

"This'll help you grow," Mrs. Morton would say whenever she left a pie at their apartment. It never seemed to work, but Darrell didn't mind because the pies were delicious.

Darrell had always been short for his age. At fifteen years old, he was just under five feet. He was also skinny, without a respectable muscle in his small body. Back in September, Darrell had dreaded starting Franklin High, but his friends were right there with him. If anyone picked on Darrell during those first weeks of school, they had the other guys to deal with too. But all that was changing.

Darrell was moving to California two months after the school year had begun. It was the first day of high school all over again, only this time Darrell did not have his friends to protect him. Darrell did not admit it to anyone, but he was scared.

"Want a cheesesteak?" Malik asked when they came to Sal's Steaks.

"I guess," Darrell said. Sal made the best cheesesteaks in the neighborhood, or maybe in the entire city. They were loaded with gobs of dripping cheese and just the right amount of fried onions.

"This one's on me," Malik said, a crack in his voice. Physically, Malik was the opposite of Darrell. He was six feet tall with big muscular shoulders. Although he was just a freshman, Malik had already earned a position on the Franklin High School varsity football team. Ever since they were young boys, Darrell was thankful that he was Malik's friend because nobody messed with Malik or his friends. Watching Malik return with the steaks, Darrell felt a wave of sadness sweep over him.

"This is our last cheesesteak together," Malik said, handing one to Darrell.

"Thanks, Malik," Darrell said. Normally, he would devour the cheesesteak quickly, but now, for the first time he could remember, he felt as if he could not eat. His throat seemed to close up on him. *It isn't fair,* he thought. Why did things happen this way? Why did he have to leave his home and his best friends? And why, of all times, did it have to be in the middle of his first year of high school? He knew why. His mother had explained it many times, but she could not change how he felt. Realizing he would hurt Malik's feelings if he did not accept his gift, Darrell forced the cheesesteak down his throat. He knew it would be the last meal he would ever have with his friend.

The boys continued walking down the darkening street. Every storefront was painful for Darrell to see. He knew he would not be back to the old neighborhood again, at least not for a long time. He glanced across the street at the old grocery store. Today it looked warm and inviting, even though the owners charged too much for meats, and the fruits and vegetables were not always fresh. At the corner, they passed the laundromat where his mother did her wash. A black mechanical rocking horse stood next to the door so parents could entertain their children while waiting for the laundry to dry. Once, Darrell and Malik gave coins to a little neighborhood kid so he could ride.

"Remember when Rasheed took four rides on our money?" Darrell asked.

"Yeah," Malik said glumly.

It was dark now. Mom had asked Darrell to be home early. The bus was leaving at 5:15 the next morning.

Darrell looked down at the emerald-green shards of a shattered beer bottle glistening in the street light. "I guess I gotta go now, Malik," he said heavily. "I gotta go home."

Home. What a mockery that word was now, Darrell thought. Home was an empty apartment with boxes in the middle of the floor, packed for the move to California. Mrs. Morton was handling the shipping for them.

"You been a real brother to me," Darrell said. "I . . . I love you, man," Darrell blurted, his voice melting into embarrassing sobs.

Malik grabbed Darrell and gave him a bear hug. For a second, Darrell's face was jammed into Malik's shirt. Then the two separated, and, without a word, started walking in opposite directions. After a few steps, Darrell began to run.

"It's not fair!" he yelled, as he sprinted through the dark. He felt as if he were being robbed, that things were being taken from him that he could never replace.

Sure, Malik would miss him, Darrell thought, but Malik was big, and he had tons of friends. Darrell was sure Malik would be fine without him.

But Darrell was not so certain about his own future. The days ahead stretched out before him like a dark road filled with dangerous shadows. It would be like the summer Mom sent him to a camp for inner-city kids. The camp director promised Darrell and his mother that he would experience adventures in the outdoors away from the dangers of the city. What Darrell ended up experiencing was torment from a kid who wanted nothing more than to make anyone weaker than him feel as miserable as possible.

The kid's name was Jermaine, and his favorite activity was torturing Darrell. He pushed Darrell into the lake. He dropped worms into Darrell's ice cream. He put laxative in Darrell's pudding, making him sick for two days. During the whole time at camp, Darrell remained silent about Jermaine. What choice did he have? He knew he did not stand a chance against Jermaine in a fight, and he knew if he told one of the adults, Jermaine would retaliate the next time no one was watching. But the biggest reason Darrell never said anything to anyone was that he was ashamed of being so helpless. At least if he kept everything to himself, no one else would know how pathetic he was. Lately, whenever Darrell thought about California, he imagined some kid like Jermaine waiting for him. Or maybe several Jermaines. And nobody would be there to help him. Not Malik. Not anyone.

As Darrell walked down the alley towards his apartment, a stray cat greeted him. It purred and rubbed its face against his calf, looking up at him with radiant green eyes.

"This is it, Max," Darrell said, petting the cat's soft gray fur. "Your last pet from me. Goodbye, Max." The cat circled his legs.

Darrell and his mother had lived in the apartment for six years. Before that, they lived in a small house. Darrell's father was with them then, but he was killed in a car accident. After his death, Darrell's mother got a job as a clerk for an insurance agency, and they moved to the apartment.

For years, everything had been fine, but then in August a larger insurance company bought out the agency where Darrell's mother worked. To save money, the company eliminated her job along with hundreds of others. For a while, she tried to find work nearby that would pay her enough to support the two of them, but the only jobs she could find were in fast-food restaurants. Then in October, Darrell's Uncle Jason, her brother, called and offered her a job in California paying twice what she could make in their neighborhood. Darrell understood why his mother chose to take the job, but he did not like her decision. *I wish he never would have called,* Darrell thought as he walked up the steps to the apartment.

"Hi, baby," his mother said as she opened the door.

Darrell tried to hurry to his room and shield his face from his mother. He did not want her to notice he had been crying.

"Are you okay?" she asked, reaching an arm out to comfort him.

"I'm fine," Darrell said, wishing she would leave him alone. He felt bad enough without his mom fussing over him.

"Oh, baby, I know how hard it is for you to leave your friends, especially in the middle of the school year. It hurts me so much to be doing this to you. If there was any other way . . ."

"It's okay," Darrell replied.

"You know if I hadn't gotten laid off—"

"Mom, I'm telling you, it's okay," Darrell insisted.

"Your Uncle Jason promising me that job in California seemed like a godsend. I got no choice," she said, putting her hand on his shoulder.

He had heard it all before, and he knew it was true. It only made Darrell angrier knowing his mother was right. If she were doing this for some selfish reason, then he could be mad at her, and it would almost feel better. "Mom, stop callin' me 'baby,' okay?"

Darrell escaped to his bedroom and sat on the bed he would use one more night. His suitcase sat alone in the middle of the floor, ready for the morning. The room where he once felt so comfortable, his cave, was no more. All his posters had been stripped from the walls.

Sitting in the dark room by himself, Darrell wanted to do something crazy, anything to avoid moving away from home. *Maybe I could run away tonight and hide in one of those empty warehouses on 35th Street*, he thought. But then he remembered his mother. There was no way he would put her through that. Instead, he stretched out on his bed and stared at the ceiling, waiting for the day to arrive.

In the morning, just before sunrise, Darrell and his mother grabbed their two suitcases and climbed aboard the westward-bound bus. Darrell stared out the window as his neighborhood passed by him for the last time. His mother talked non-stop in a nervous monologue. Darrell paid little attention.

"Darrell, just give it a chance. You might like California. Uncle Jason said our new neighborhood is much nicer than here. He said the houses are well kept, and we'll be close to the stadium, and you can see baseball and football games."

Darrell closed his eyes and resolved to hate California no matter what anybody said.

"Jason also said the school you'll be going to is pretty new. It's an old neighborhood, but the school is only about fifteen years old. It's called Bluford High. It's named for an African American astronaut," his mother went on.

Darrell closed his eyes and said nothing. He knew his silence would hurt his mother's feelings. But he could not help it. Nothing she could say would convince him that he'd like California.

"Oh, honey," she added, "if you'd just give it a chance."

Darrell sank deeper into his seat.

"I hated to leave my friends too, Darrell," she continued. "I made some wonderful friends at the office and on our street, and I won't know anybody in California either except for my brother and his family."

It's different with you, Mom, Darrell thought. *You make friends easily. I'll be in class with kids who've gone through middle school together and had two months in high school to get used to each other. They'll see this kid from Philadelphia who looks twelve years old, and I'm in for it.* Yet he said nothing. He did not feel like explaining things to his mother. She would only worry about him even more.

"Just put a big, friendly smile on your face your first day there, honey, and by the end of the day you'll have at least one nice friend," she said.

Maybe that worked in first grade when everybody was wearing name tags and kids hadn't learned to be mean to each other yet, Darrell thought. But kids learn fast. By third grade, Darrell was glad he had Malik, Big Reggie, and Mark.

But now, he wouldn't have anybody.

Everything Darrell knew and loved was gone. And though she meant well, his mother had no idea how hard it was to be the new kid in school, especially one who is smaller than everyone else.

Darrell remembered that his Uncle Jason was well over six feet tall. A few years ago, he came to Philadelphia to visit, and he looked at then twelve-year-old Darrell and said in a booming voice, "Will you look at that boy? Why is he so skinny? Nobody in our family was ever that small at his age! Jackie, ain't you feedin' him enough?"

His mother seemed defensive. "Oh, he'll hit his growth spurt anytime now," she said, "He'll shoot up like a spring weed. Then you won't even recognize him, Jason."

Remembering that conversation, Darrell could only think one thing—his mother was wrong.

She refused to accept the truth, Darrell thought. And the truth was that he was still a short, underweight kid, and all the hopes and smiles in the world were not going to change that.

Darrell gazed out the window while the bus raced farther and farther from his home. A feeling of dread weighed heavily on him as the sun crawled slowly into the sky.

Chapter 2

When the bus stopped at a roadside diner for lunch, Darrell saw a Mustang parked nearby. Loud rap music pounded from the car's open windows.

You tell me to be a man,
But you don't understand,
You ain't lived this life,
You ain't paid this price,
You ain't had these blues,
Try walkin' in my shoes.

Passing the Mustang on his way into the diner, Darrell made eye contact with one of the boys in the car. Darrell tried to work his face into a smile, just like his mother said to do. But the guy in the Mustang did not seem to like a short, skinny kid smiling at him. He glared at Darrell with a menacing look that seemed to ask, *"What's your problem, fool?"*

Inside the diner, Darrell could not eat the bacon cheeseburger he had ordered.

"Darrell," his mother urged, "eat your burger. It looks good."

He was not hungry. He did not have the heart to tell his mother that the burger tasted like cardboard and the bacon strips felt like pieces of salty leather on his tongue.

Back inside the bus, Darrell stared glumly out the window and watched the miles roll by. For three days, they lumbered across the country, stopping only to eat and change buses. Occasionally, his mother would point out interesting things she'd see out the window—mountains, rivers, an odd building. The whole time, Darrell sulked. He knew, with each passing mile, that his home was farther away and his new neighborhood—and a new high school—were getting closer.

Darrell's first look at California was of a desert rimmed by the chocolate-colored Laguna Mountains. Beyond them was a lush valley where reddish-brown horses and a few large cows grazed. Big houses with red-tiled roofs sat on mesas. Darrell could hardly believe people actually lived like that. He wondered what Malik would say if he saw such a place.

As they entered the city, the landscape changed. Older stucco houses were crowded on narrow lots, with newer apartments stuck here and there along the street. Before long, the bus pulled to a stop next to a trolley station. Darrell and his mother grabbed their suitcases and hobbled off the bus to a bench outside the station. Almost immediately, Darrell's Uncle Jason pulled up in his truck.

"Hey, Jackie!" Uncle Jason bellowed as he hopped out of the truck. "I'll bet you're worn out from that long trip."

Darrell looked at his uncle with awe. He had rippling muscles and a barrel chest. He looked even taller than Darrell remembered.

"Well, I could sure use a hot bath and a good night's sleep," his mother admitted wearily, hugging her brother.

Uncle Jason turned to Darrell, seizing him in a massive embrace that lifted his feet off the ground. "Good to see you again, Darrell," he said. Darrell could tell his uncle was looking at how small he was. "We're gonna grow you, boy," he added. "We're gonna make sure you get what you need to grow into the big strong boy the good Lord intended you to be."

Darrell felt ridiculous. His uncle treated him like a turkey that needed to be fattened up for Thanksgiving. He had never liked Uncle Jason. He had always been too loud, too pushy.

"The apartment is all set for you, Jackie," Uncle Jason said, loading their bags into the back of the truck. "It's furnished too. Your stuff arrived this morning. You got a bedroom, and there's one for the boy."

When Darrell and Mom were settled in the truck, Uncle Jason closed the back door, got into the driver's seat, and pulled out into traffic.

"You're so good to be doing all this for us, Jason," Mom said.

"Well, we're family. That's what families do. Besides, ever since Lewis died, I thought I should step in and look out for Darrell. I'm glad I have you all where I can see you." At a stoplight, Uncle Jason turned around and gave Darrell a friendly jab in the chest. "There's your new high school. Bluford High. They got some fine sports teams there, Darrell. As soon as you get big and strong, you'll be wearin' a jersey with your name on it. You'll see."

17

Darrell knew his uncle did not mean to insult him, but he was doing it just the same. Darrell did not think he would ever be big enough for football or basketball, and he was not coordinated enough for baseball either. He wished his Uncle Jason would just shut up.

"You wanna build up your muscles, Darrell, do push-ups, run, whatever it takes," he said. "You are gonna have to work extra hard, though, 'cause your arms are really skinny. You look like you could get hurt if somebody tried to high-five you." Uncle Jason shook his head and chuckled to himself.

"Oh, Darrell is getting more height and weight every day," his mother said.

Darrell tried to tune out their voices—his mother's pathetic, false hopes that he would someday become a tall athlete, and his uncle's insulting advice about getting bigger.

Trying to ignore their conversation, Darrell could think of only one thing—he hated California already. He *hated* it.

"This is our neighborhood," announced Uncle Jason after a while. Two boys were standing in front of a sandwich shop at a street corner. One wore a Los Angeles Dodgers baseball cap backwards.

That is how Malik always wore his baseball cap. The kid was built like Malik too—big and burly. He even leaned against the wall like Malik used to, one leg crossed at a funny angle. A bolt of sadness shot through Darrell.

Darrell imagined the kid *was* Malik, and he could hear their conversation in his mind.

"Malik, you ain't ever gonna believe my uncle. He's makin' me feel ten times worse about my size. Yet he keeps thinkin' that he's helping me. All he does is tell me how small I am."

"Man, don't listen to him," Malik would say. *"He's jealous 'cause you're so young and he's so old. Next time he says somethin' to you, tell him to mind his own business. Anyone who sounds as dumb as him has no right to be givin' you advice, you hear me?"*

Darrell smiled weakly. He had always felt better when he talked to Malik. Even imagining what Malik would say raised his spirits.

"Here we are," Uncle Jason said, snapping Darrell out of his daydream. He pulled into the small driveway of a stucco duplex. Uncle Jason and his family occupied the three-bedroom unit in front, and

Darrell and his mother would live in the rear unit. Everything looked neat and clean, and multi-colored flowers had been planted along the walkway.

"Come on, Darrell," his mother yelled as they got out of the truck. "We're home. This is home now."

No, he thought, *this isn't home. Not my home.*

She walked over to him, put her arm around his shoulders, and rubbed his back. "Just be patient," she said. "You'll learn to like it here."

As Darrell carried his suitcase towards the back unit, a boy came running out of Uncle Jason's house. He was a meaty boy, big for his age. He looked just like his father. "Hey, you must be my cousin Darrell," the boy said. "I'm Travis. I'm nine. How old are you?"

Darrell had almost forgotten that his uncle had two sons. The last time he saw them was at his father's funeral.

"I'm fifteen," Darrell said.

"No way! You ain't fifteen. I'm almost as tall as you are. How come you're so short?" Travis demanded, dribbling a basketball as he ran alongside Darrell. "Huh? Why are you so short?"

Then Uncle Jason's other son, Nate,

appeared. Nate was almost three years younger than Travis. Darrell tried to ignore the boys as they dodged in front of him with the basketball.

"How tall are you?" Travis asked. "I'm gonna be bigger than you soon."

Before Darrell could answer, his uncle came out of the duplex and went up to the boy. Pretending to be an opposing basketball player, he quickly knocked the ball from Travis's hands. "You gotta be fast, boy," he said, putting his hand on his son's head. "Now go help your momma with dinner, or you won't get no dessert, hear?" He laughed then, shaking his head as the two kids sprinted inside. It was clear to Darrell that he was bursting with pride over them. "Those boys of mine are something else. When they get a little older, they're gonna be the best basketball players this town ever saw. Man, they been dribbling since they learned to walk!"

Darrell went to his room and started unpacking. He had just finished putting his favorite Allen Iverson poster on the wall when his mother poked her head in the door.

"All unpacked, honey?" she asked.

"Almost, Mom," he answered, trying not to sound sad.

"I'm going over to the office with your uncle. He's going to show me where I'm going to work and introduce me to everybody. Will you be okay?"

"Sure," Darrell mumbled.

Darrell waited until his mother was gone. There were still a couple of hours of daylight, and he thought he would walk down the street and check out the neighborhood.

Darrell headed for the shopping plaza at the corner. He tried to look cool, walking calmly as if he knew where he was going but was in no particular hurry to get there. Malik and his friends had that kind of walk down to a fine art. They moved as if they owned the street and could handle anything that came along. They were not menacing, but no one wanted to mess with them. Most people would look the other way whenever Malik walked down the street.

Darrell caught his reflection in a store window as he walked. He reminded himself of a rat scurrying down an alley, hoping no cats could see him. He figured that to the rest of the world he looked like a little kid afraid of his own shadow.

Ahead there were five boys in front of a small sandwich shop. They looked to be around fifteen or sixteen years old, and each of them was bigger than Darrell. They did not look like the tough kids he knew of back home. Instead they seemed like ordinary guys just hanging out, the way he and his friends did. Two had soda cans and were shoving each other and laughing. Malik and Reggie used to do the same thing. Darrell wondered if any of the boys were freshmen at Bluford.

He thought about what to do. *Wouldn't it be something if I smiled and introduced myself, and they turned out to be friendly guys,* he said to himself. *Maybe they're just like Malik, Reggie, and Mark. If I get to know them, the first day at Bluford won't be so bad.*

Darrell moved closer and tried his mother's advice. He smiled at the group of guys, trying to hide the fact that his bony knees were almost knocking together.

"What are you laughin' at, fool?" the biggest boy called out. He was almost as tall and muscular as Malik. "You think we're funny or somethin'?"

"No, no," Darrell said quickly, his mind spinning, searching for the right words. *It was easy to talk to Malik and the guys back home, but these guys are different,* Darrell thought. He had no idea what to say to them. "I'm . . . new around here," he mumbled nervously, "and I'm going to Buford."

"*Buford?* What's that? You stupid or something?" the big one demanded as his friends laughed almost on cue.

"I . . . I mean *Bluford*," Darrell stammered, "yeah . . . Bluford."

"Why didn't you say that in the first place? You got some kinda speech problem?" the big one asked. "Anyhow, you ain't foolin' nobody. You some sixth grader tryin' to pretend you're in high school." He stepped so close that Darrell could smell his breath, a sickening mixture of onions and cigarette smoke. "What's your name, kid?" he asked.

"I'm Darrell . . . Mercer."

"Darrell . . . Mercer," the boy repeated with a chuckle.

Darrell's name struck them all as funny. They kept saying it over and over in a mocking way. Darrell looked for a way to get away from them, but he was surrounded. Finally, the big kid asked, "You got any money on you, Darrell Mercer?"

"For what?" Darrell asked.

"We thought you'd make us a loan, so we don't put your scrawny butt in that trash dumpster over there," the big one said. His friends started laughing out loud. One kid in an oversized Lakers shirt doubled over, unable to control his laughter.

"He looks like he's going to wet his pants," the kid in the Lakers shirt said, struggling to catch his breath amidst his laughter.

Darrell gave them $3.25, all he had. His hands were trembling when he turned over the money.

"Three bucks? That all you got?" the muscular kid demanded. Darrell stared at him in open-mouthed terror. Then, without a word, Darrell tried to walk down the sidewalk past them, but they all moved into his path, blocking him. The large kid raised his finger and poked Darrell's chest. "I'm Tyray Hobbs. I'm a freshman at Bluford, and I run things around here. Hear what I'm sayin'?"

"Yeah," Darrell said, nodding his head. He wanted to go home, not to Uncle Jason's, but back to Philadelphia. Once again, he tried to move down the sidewalk. This time, the boys stepped aside. But as he hurried to get past them, Tyray stuck his foot out. Unable to step over Tyray's Nikes, Darrell tripped and fell into the gutter. His teeth jammed into his lip when he hit the ground. He could taste the salty blood oozing into his mouth.

"You clumsy or what?" Tyray asked.

"You some kind fool or something?" another boy asked.

Darrell got slowly to his feet. The cut in his mouth was small. He hid it by sucking in his bottom lip. He did not want anyone to see he was bleeding.

So this is how it's gonna be, Darrell thought.

"Look at him shakin'," Tyray bragged, and they all laughed again, the sound like car horns in a rush-hour traffic jam.

Darrell turned around and started walking slowly back towards his new apartment.

A young couple pushing a baby stroller were coming towards him. The man was burly. Darrell figured Tyray and his friends would not mess with them. When he got about ten feet from the baby stroller, he looked back. The boys were gone.

Tyray and his friends had slipped back into the shadows, but Darrell knew he would see them again. When he arrived at Bluford High, they would be there, walking the halls, sitting in the locker room, hanging out in the gym.

They would be waiting for him.

That night, Darrell listened to his mother talk excitedly about her new job as a secretary at Uncle Jason's office. She had fixed Darrell's favorite dinner—fried chicken, mashed potatoes with plenty of thick brown gravy, and a big salad with crisp lettuce and tomatoes. "It's such a nice place, honey," she said. "The construction workers come in, and they are so friendly. Mostly I just need to talk to people. I use the computer a little bit too."

"Sounds great, Mom," Darrell said. There was no way he was going to tell her what had happened. He did not have the heart to ruin her first day in California. Besides, he thought, all she would tell him to do was smile. *Look where that got me,* he thought.

That night Darrell could not sleep. Even though it was quiet, he could still hear the sound of laughter, Tyray's laughter.

And all Darrell could think about was that this was just the beginning.

Chapter 3

On the following Sunday, before Darrell's first day at Bluford, his mother asked him to walk to the supermarket to pick up some groceries. She said the store was only four blocks away. Darrell was nervous about going out again, but it was early Sunday, so he thought everything might be okay. To be safe, Darrell made sure that Tyray and his friends were nowhere in sight before he headed down the street.

The supermarket was nicer than the one back home. The aisles were cleaner, and the vegetables did not look as old and limp as they did in Philadelphia. Some things were the same, though—security guards were posted at the doors to stop people from stealing, and the lines seemed long and slow. After Darrell gathered all the things on his mother's list, he moved to the nearest checkout. In front of him was a pretty girl reading a magazine. Darrell noticed she was wearing a snug blue T-shirt with the words *Bluford High Buccaneers* printed on the back. The image of a pirate's face with a patch over his eye filled the rest of her back.

Darrell's heart raced. Here was a chance to meet a girl from Bluford. He wanted desperately to say "hi," but he did not know what he would say after that. He did not want to make a fool of himself. He had decided it would be better to keep quiet when she suddenly looked up from her magazine and smiled.

"Hi," she said.

"Hi," Darrell said in a voice barely above a whisper. The girl had warm brown eyes and a friendly smile. She was a bit taller than he was. Most girls his age were. He thought it would be great to be friends with her, but he still could not think of anything to say. He wondered what Malik would do in his shoes.

"I shoulda known not to come in on Sunday morning," she said. "That's when everyone does their shopping, and the lines take forever. I can't stand being stuck here doing nothing." She put the magazine back in the rack.

"Yeah, I know what you mean. The other day I took a bus ride that lasted for three days. I almost went crazy sitting still that long," Darrell said.

"You traveled that long just to get *here*?" she said, seeming surprised. "Where are you from?"

"Philadelphia. My mom and I moved 'cause she got a good job out here. Tomorrow I start school at Bluford," he said.

"Really?" This time she seemed almost shocked.

She probably thinks I look too young to be in high school, Darrell thought.

"Yeah, I'm a freshman," he said, trying to hide his annoyance.

"I thought you looked like one," she laughed. "So am I. I guess we freshmen have sort of a look about us, no matter where we're from."

"We freshmen." Darrell turned the phrase over in his mind. He liked it because of the word *we.* It meant he was not alone. At least not as alone as he was before she said it. He held on to that simple phrase the way a drowning person clutches a rope.

"So, what's your name?" she asked.

"Darrell Mercer," he replied.

"Well hello, Darrell Mercer," she said. "I'm Amberlynn Bailey." She smiled and reached her hand out to shake his.

He took her hand. It was warm and soft. For a second, he forgot about the fact that he had lost all his friends, and that Tyray would be waiting for him at Bluford tomorrow.

Finally the line moved, and Amberlynn turned around to pack her groceries. For once, Darrell wished that the checkout line was even slower.

"Well, see you at school, Darrell," she said, handing money to the cashier. "Maybe we've got classes together."

"That'd be cool," he said.

Walking home, Darrell felt a little better about California. Amberlynn was really nice. Maybe there were other kids at Bluford like her. Maybe it'd be okay after all. Tyray and his friends might not be in any of his classes. They might even forget all about him. Darrell hoped there would be someone like Malik in Bluford.

Carrying three heavy bags of groceries home, Darrell mumbled, "Maybe the exercise will help build up my muscles." As he neared the driveway, he could hear the sound of a basketball being dribbled

31

against the concrete. Turning the corner, he saw his cousin Travis taking shots at the basket near the edge of the driveway.

"What are you doin' carrying all those bags?" Travis asked.

"I just went to the store to get groceries," Darrell replied, walking quickly past the boy.

"When we go to the store, we take my Dad's new truck. It's a Nissan. What kind of car does your mom drive?"

Darrell hesitated. He wasn't sure if Travis knew that they did not own a car. He didn't want to admit the truth to him.

"We left our car in Philly because one of our friends needed it," he said, walking up the stairs of the new apartment.

"Are you and your momma poor?" Travis asked. "My daddy says you were poor people in Philadelphia and that's why he brought you here. 'Cause you couldn't take care of yourselves," the boy added, watching Darrell closely.

Darrell took a deep breath, trying to contain the anger that suddenly boiled in his chest. *Would Uncle Jason say such a thing? He must have said something,* Darrell thought, *because no nine-year-old kid would say something like that on his own. Not unless he was mean. Real mean.*

"We ain't poor, and it ain't any of your business what we are. Now, I gotta put these groceries away," Darrell said, fuming. As he turned to open the apartment door, Nate came outside. The young boy said he wanted to shoot baskets with his brother.

"You're too short to play basketball," Travis said, holding the ball over Nate's head so the boy could not reach it.

"Gimme the ball, gimme the ball," Nate begged, but Travis kept it just out of his brother's reach. Darrell looked away and went inside.

When he walked in, his mother stopped unpacking boxes and came over to help him put the groceries away.

"You okay about school tomorrow, honey?" she asked.

"I'm okay," Darrell said.

"You know it's only a mile down to Bluford. And when it rains, you can catch the bus right out on the corner."

"I know, Mom."

"I'll pack you a nice sandwich and an orange—"

"No, Mom. I'll get something in the cafeteria." He could tell she was worried about him and that this was her way of telling him she cared. But it bothered him when she treated him like a baby. It only made him feel smaller. He wished she would just leave him alone.

"Well, just in case, I'll put some granola bars in your backpack," his mother said, opening her purse and fishing out ten dollars. "Here you go, honey."

He felt bad taking the money. Back in Philadelphia, he would occasionally find work to make a few dollars. Once in a while he baby-sat a neighbor's kid. A few times he worked at a small pizza shop sweeping the floors, keeping the counters clean, and taking out the trash. Sometimes he even made enough to give some money to his mother. "Maybe I'll find a job here, Mom. You know, like the ones I had back home," he said.

"Don't you worry, honey," she replied. "I'm making better money now. You just concentrate on school."

As his mother spoke, Darrell heard a muffled yell come from outside. He walked to the door and looked out to see Travis and Nate fighting in the driveway. Nate was lying on his stomach. His arm was twisted behind his back, and Travis was straddling him, saying, "Say you're sorry. You better say it, or I'll twist it harder. Say it." Nate was whimpering.

Dirt and pieces of leaves were in his hair. He was struggling, but he was unable to escape his bigger brother.

Darrell could not bear to watch. He knew how Nate felt. He had been in that position before. He remembered the times Jermaine hurt him and no one stepped in to help. No matter where he went, it seemed there always were bigger kids who liked to show how strong they were by picking on smaller, weaker people. Now he was seeing the same thing happening in his own family. He could not sit still and let it happen.

Darrell bolted out of the apartment, jumped down the steps, and moved in behind Travis. Then in one quick motion, he wrapped his arms around Travis's chest and yanked the larger boy off his brother. Stunned, Travis kicked and squirmed until Darrell let go.

"Keep your hands off me!" Travis yelled.

"Pick on someone your own size next time," Darrell said. His pulse was pounding.

"I'm gonna tell my dad what you did!" Travis screamed, enraged that Darrell had interfered.

The yelling drew Uncle Jason from

the house. "Hey, what's the problem here?" he asked.

"Darrell is pushin' me around. He said he's gonna hurt me," Travis whined.

"Tell me what's goin' on, Darrell. What are you doin' messin' with my boy?" Uncle Jason asked.

"Travis was beating up Nate, so I stopped it. I didn't hurt him," Darrell said.

Uncle Jason started smiling and nodding before Darrell finished his sentence. His face seemed to brighten, as if something pleased him. "Those boys like to play a little rough, Darrell. That's part of a boy's growin' up that you been missing out on. I'm hopin' living here with us will give you a little of what you've been missing." He threw an arm around Darrell's shoulders. "Don't worry when you see the boys playin' rough. They're just testin' themselves. That's how a boy becomes a man. Understand?"

Darrell said nothing. Uncle Jason walked over to his sons, holding his fists up near his face like a fighter in a boxing match. Then he stepped closer and faked slow-motion punches into the boys' chests, stopping just before his fist reached them. "You boys get inside and get cleaned up. Go on!" he said. He put his big hand on their shoulders and gently steered them towards the front door. Travis grinned at his father, but Darrell noticed a different look in Nate's eyes. The little boy was rubbing the arm Travis had twisted, and though he said nothing, Darrell could read the look as if it were a word written on a sheet of paper. There was hatred in Nate's face.

Darrell knew that feeling well. *Poor Nate*, he thought. He decided he would watch out for his little cousin, no matter what his uncle said. That was what Malik would do. And that was what he was going to do too.

Chapter 4

Sunday night, Darrell had trouble sleeping. Every few hours he woke up and checked the clock to see how much time he had left to rest. He wanted the night to last forever. At least then he would not have to go to school. Yet every time he looked at the clock, it was closer and closer to the time he had to get up, the time he had to go to the same place as Tyray. Alone.

Darrell was awake when the day's first dim light started to creep into his small bedroom. The weather seemed to match his mood. A raw November rain left the sky dull gray and sunless. *What a day to begin at Bluford,* he thought.

For breakfast, he forced himself to eat a few spoonfuls of oatmeal and a gulp of milk.

"Darrell," his mother scolded, "that's

not enough to keep a bird alive. How you gonna grow taller and heavier if you eat like that?"

"I can't eat no more, Mom. My stomach feels funny already," Darrell said.

"Poor baby. You're really nervous about school, huh? I'm so sorry we had to make the move out here after school started . . . I know you wanted to stay at Franklin back home." She came over and kissed him on the top of his head. Though part of him hated that she felt the need to baby him, another part of him was glad she did it—as long as it was in private. It was comforting to know how much his mom loved him, and he clung to that when things got really bad. Just as long as she never babied him in front of anybody.

Even though the sky was dreary and rain seemed to be lurking in the swollen clouds, Darrell chose to walk to school. After the long bus trip from Philadelphia, he preferred to walk in the rain rather than sit on another bus, even if the ride lasted only a few minutes.

At 7:30, he grabbed his backpack and headed out to the street. Just in case Tyray was waiting for him, Darrell walked off the main route, sticking instead to a back street that went in the same direction.

As he neared the school, Darrell saw more and more kids. He glanced at the different groups of people all around him, hoping to see someone his own size, a freshman looking more like a middle-schooler. Finally as he reached the front of the school, he spotted a little guy with glasses. He was stockier than Darrell, but just as short. Darrell quickened his pace to catch up to him, figuring that at least they could share their misery over being so small. But as Darrell watched, two other boys walked up alongside of the smaller kid.

"Hey, Jamel. How's it goin'?" one boy asked.

The smaller boy turned and smiled. "Wassup, Miguel?"

The third spoke up then. "Jamel, did Mitchell cover anything important on Friday? I missed class."

"We did Act III of *Romeo and Juliet*. You can borrow my notes," Jamel replied.

"Man, what kinda story is that? Makes me glad I don't have a girlfriend," said Miguel.

The three continued talking and laughing. Darrell figured they had probably been friends all their lives—just like he had been with Malik, Reggie, and Mark.

The short kid with the glasses is nothing like me, he thought. Jamel was "in." Darrell was on the outside looking in. Disappointed and alone, Darrell kept walking. Everyone was talking to somebody else. All the kids around him seemed to be with old friends. Everything Darrell had feared was coming true. He was probably the only new kid in the entire school.

Darrell's first class was English. It took him a few minutes to figure out where the room was. As he walked in, he noticed a familiar face. Amberlynn was in his class! Grateful to see someone he recognized, Darrell looked for a seat next to her, but they were all filled. A few other girls were talking to her when he came in, and she did not seem to notice him.

Anyway, why would she want me to sit next to her when she can have all her friends nearby? Darrell thought. Besides, he had to be careful not to take someone else's seat. He did not want to make enemies on his first day. He decided to take the nearest empty seat but then saw a kid in the back of the room motioning for him. The boy was pointing to a desk next to him. Darrell thought the guy was being friendly, but as he sat down at the desk, he recognized the boy's face. He was one of the kids with Tyray the other day. Darrell turned to get up when he saw something that made his jaw drop.

Tyray walked into the classroom.

Quickly scanning the class, Tyray strolled over to the boy who sat next to Darrell and gave him a high five. "Wassup, Rodney," Tyray said. Then, walking behind Darrell's desk, Tyray kicked it, jarring Darrell and causing the whole desk to move a few inches. "Whoops," Tyray said as he sat down in the desk on the other side of Darrell.

Darrell felt trapped. He could not imagine how he would survive a whole year with Tyray and Rodney on either side of him.

Just then the teacher, Mr. Mitchell, came in. He stepped behind his desk at the front of the room and surveyed the class through dark wire-rimmed glasses. Darrell was relieved he was there. It meant he was safe, at least for the moment.

"We have a transfer student all the way from Philadelphia joining the class today," Mr. Mitchell said. "His name is Darrell Mercer." As the teacher spoke, everyone in the class turned to look at Darrell. He wanted to hide under his desk. He could feel their eyes scanning him. He knew they were thinking he looked too short to be in high school, that he looked skinny and weak. Worse, he thought, maybe some were feeling sorry for him because of how small and scared he looked. He wanted to get up and run out of the class. Instead he just waited in agony for the stares to go away. "Darrell," Mr. Mitchell continued, "are you sure you want to sit in the back of the class? I'm not always nice to people who sit in the back row." He smiled as he spoke. Then he turned to erase some writing off the chalkboard.

This is my chance, Darrell thought. *A chance to get away from Tyray and Rodney.* "I guess I could see better from the front," Darrell replied. As he started to get up, Darrell felt a sharp pain in his shoulder. Tyray's wide hand gripped his small shoulder like a giant claw and shoved him back into his seat.

"You ain't goin' nowhere, fool," Tyray whispered. The whole time, Tyray looked straight ahead, making sure not to draw Mr. Mitchell's attention. Only nearby kids seemed to notice the drama unfolding in the back of the classroom. When Darrell looked at them for help, they just looked the other way.

"I can, uh . . . see better from up there," Darrell pleaded quietly to Tyray.

"How much you gonna be able to see when I punch your face so hard your eyes swell shut?"

Darrell always thought teachers were fools. They never seemed to know what was going on in their classrooms. Kids could be hiding drugs or threatening other kids, and the teachers would just ramble on about some poem written hundreds of years ago. Mr. Mitchell seemed worse because Tyray had actually touched Darrell right in front of him, and he still did not notice.

"We still have this empty desk up front," Mr. Mitchell said, "and it looks like Darrell doesn't want it. But, you know, it hurts my feelings to see such a good spot in the front of the room go to waste. So I am going to give it to a very lucky person today. Tyray, you are the winner. Why don't you move up here?"

"Why me?" Tyray growled. "I didn't do nothin'!"

"The back of the room seems a bit too distracting for you. Besides, people who sit in the front of the room tend to have much better grade point averages than those who sit in the back. So come on up here," he said.

A few kids in the classroom laughed. Darrell held his breath. He wanted Tyray to move as far away from him as possible.

"I ain't movin' from here," Tyray said in a sullen voice.

"You're on the freshman football team, aren't you, Tyray?" Mr. Mitchell asked.

"Yeah," Tyray mumbled, crossing his arms on his chest. "So?"

"Well, Coach Meade and I are good friends. And I would hate to have to tell him that you refused to listen to a teacher. He might think you would refuse to listen on the football field. He might even kick you off the team. Now if you want to avoid all that, why don't you just sit up front?"

Tyray slowly got to his feet. On his way towards the front of the classroom, he deliberately stepped on Darrell's foot. Pain shot like electricity through Darrell's body. "Whoops, sorry," Tyray said, acting as innocent as possible. Despite the pain, Darrell felt great relief. At least he did not have to sit next to Tyray. He also had respect for his new English teacher. Darrell was not exactly sure if Mr. Mitchell knew what Tyray was doing to him in the back of the room, but it did not matter. Without embarrassing Darrell, Mr. Mitchell had managed to stop what was happening. And for that Darrell was grateful.

As lunchtime drew near, Darrell started to feel a new kind of anxiety. He worried that he would eat lunch alone. When the bell rang, he walked reluctantly towards the cafeteria, dreading the meal to come. Inside, he took his place at the end of the line, got his plastic tray, and slowly moved towards where the kitchen staff dished out the food. The menu for the day was spaghetti and meatballs, along with a piece of garlic bread and a scoop of green beans. Dessert was a soupy green gelatin with strange-looking pieces of fruit suspended inside it.

Just like the school cafeteria back home, Darrell thought.

When his tray was full, Darrell stepped into the rapidly filling lunch area. *Is there anyone I can sit with?* he wondered. Before him, hundreds of people talked, laughed and ate with their friends. No one seemed as lost as he was. He spotted two freshman guys sitting nearby at a table with two empty chairs. Darrell had seen them in his morning classes. He wondered if he should try to go over and join them. They seemed friendly enough.

Darrell carried his full tray towards them. In his mind, he rehearsed what would happen next.

"Anybody sitting here?" he would ask.

"No, sit down, man," they'd say.

Then Darrell would have his foot in the door. They'd talk about classes, their teachers. Then they'd make fun of the cafeteria food and talk about the best-looking girls in the school. The ice would be broken.

Even though he was nervous, he decided to try what he had rehearsed. He went over to the table with the two freshmen, his knees shaking the whole way.

"Uh, anybody sitting here?" Darrell asked.

They did not respond the way they did in his mind. They did not even look up. Were they ignoring him? He felt ridiculous standing there with a full tray talking to people who were paying no

47

attention to him. They continued their conversation as if he did not exist. *Maybe they didn't hear me,* he thought. He tried again in a louder voice.

"Anybody sitting here?"

This time one of the boys looked up. "Yeah. We're saving the places for friends."

"Sorry," Darrell said, embarrassed. Quickly he moved away from the table.

You stupid fool, Darrell thought. He imagined them laughing about him, chuckling at the scrawny kid who tried to sit at their table.

Again Darrell looked out over the cafeteria. It was filled with hundreds of kids his age. But for him it was empty. Standing amidst the huge crowd, Darrell felt more alone than he ever had in his whole life.

Darrell remembered being with his old friends in middle school. They were a single unit. Four boys, four separate people, but they were really one. What if a new kid came along and tried to join their special group? Would they have welcomed him? Probably not. Malik might have looked at the stranger and said the same thing, *"We're saving that place for a friend."* It would not have been that they were bad guys. It was just how things were.

Get used to it, Darrell thought. Finally he spotted an empty table over in the corner. He quickly moved to it the way people in a rainstorm run for cover. Alone, he shoved a tangled mass of soggy spaghetti noodles into his mouth. The food was bad too, he thought. The spaghetti sauce tasted like red paste, and the gelatin dessert had an odd chemical flavor.

He hoped that some other lonely student would join him, but nobody came.

Darrell wondered what his friends back home were doing right now. At Franklin, they'd eat lunch in a table near a window. It was a great place to eat, and whoever got to the cafeteria first raced to claim it. From their table, they could see people passing by on the street below. Darrell and Malik liked to point out attractive girls as they walked by the school. He wondered if they even noticed he was gone.

Suddenly Darrell was aware of two guys standing at his table. For a minute, he thought they'd come to join him. He looked up at them and smiled, trying to be as friendly as possible.

"You done?" one of the guys asked.

The question hit Darrell like a slap in the face. Instantly he realized his mistake. The boys knew he was done eating, and they wanted his table. Not him, his *table*.

"Oh yeah," Darrell said, picking up his tray and walking over to the trash barrel. He dumped his plastic dishes and stacked the tray. Before he walked out of the cafeteria, he paused for a second and looked back at the crowd behind him.

It was amazing, he thought. He had spent the entire morning in classes with so many kids. But not one joined him for lunch. Would he spend the whole year at Bluford alone?

Chapter 5

During algebra class, Darrell was sure Amberlynn looked right at him. He knew she did. She was only about five feet away. But then she looked away as if she had never seen him before. Didn't she remember standing in the line at the supermarket? Didn't she remember saying "we freshmen" as if they had a special bond? Clearly their conversation was not as important to her as it was to him.

Just behind Amberlynn was a heavyset boy who seemed to nod at Darrell at the beginning of class. When the teacher, Ms. Webb, took attendance, Darrell learned the boy's name was Harold Davis. But during the rest of the class, the boy did not look in his direction. Darrell figured he must have imagined that Harold was trying to be friendly.

Once Ms. Webb started teaching, the class passed pretty quickly. Darrell was glad he was able to understand the day's lesson. But like lunch, the algebra class ended without a single person bothering to talk to him.

After algebra, Darrell went to his last class, the one he feared most—gym class. Darrell knew he looked small enough with regular clothes on, but in gym shorts and a T-shirt, he felt ridiculous. He went into the locker room and got ready to change into the gym clothes he brought from home. He could not stand having other kids see him shirtless, so he waited until most of them had gone before he changed. When he came out of the locker room, he sat with the other kids and waited for Mr. Dooling, the teacher, to take attendance. Mr. Dooling was a tall balding white man who looked to be in his mid-fifties. He looked like he spent his entire teaching career in the Bluford gymnasium.

"Listen up, freshmen," Mr. Dooling instructed. "Before we get started, I want to make a few announcements. First of all, the fall season is almost over. This means winter sports teams will start soon. I encourage you all to join a winter sport—indoor track, basketball, or wrestling. Sports help you build strength, discipline, and confidence," he said. A few people in the class snickered. Darrell thought about each of the sports and decided there was no way he would ever try to play a sport at Bluford. Not in a million years.

Then it happened again. Mr. Dooling told the class that they had a new student from Philadelphia and asked him to stand up. Embarrassed, Darrell stood, the only kid forced to do so in the entire gym class.

"Man, that boy looks like he should join the wrestling team. He could be the practice dummy," someone whispered nearby. A few kids laughed.

"He looks like a chicken. Look at them chicken legs," said another voice. When he turned to face them, everyone just looked at him with straight faces.

"Welcome to Bluford, Darrell," Mr. Dooling said. The teacher was too far away to hear the kids' comments.

"Thanks," Darrell said, sitting down. "Thanks a lot," he mumbled.

The gym assignment was to jog outside, loop around the track four times, and run back in. "If you like this run,"

Mr. Dooling said, "go out for winter track."

Darrell followed the crowd outside and began to jog. About halfway around the track, he heard a familiar voice behind him.

"Hey, chicken legs. You're in sorry shape."

He turned back to see Tyray and Rodney running side by side. Darrell nearly stumbled over his own feet when he saw them. He felt like a cat being chased by a pack of wild dogs. But for him, there was no tree to climb. Fortunately, Mr. Dooling was jogging along with the class, and he was not far away. Darrell decided to stick with Mr. Dooling's pace, no matter how fast he ran. "Boy, you are going to hate Bluford," Tyray said. Then he started to pass Darrell. As he went by, he stepped on the heel of Darrell's shoe, almost causing him to trip. "Hey, man, watch where you're stepping," he added as he sprinted ahead.

Darrell's spirits were never lower. He did not know how he was going to survive the whole year this way. A year without friends would be bad enough. But a year with Tyray would be unbearable. At the end of gym, Darrell changed as quickly as possible. He wanted to get out of the locker room before Tyray bumped into him again. When the bell finally rang, Darrell moved quickly through the hallways and out of Bluford. *Thank God the day is over,* he thought.

Darrell decided to go home using the same route he took to school, through a back street instead of the main street. As he walked behind the supermarket, he noticed Amberlynn walking with a friend not far ahead of him. The other girl was Jamee Wills, also in his English class. Neither girl seemed to pay any attention to him. They were busy talking about their day and their plans for the evening. After a minute, Jamee turned off in another direction, and Amberlynn was alone. Immediately she walked over to join him.

Darrell looked at her as she approached him. Her eyes were dark brown, almost black, and her skin was the color of milk chocolate. He noticed how her body curved gracefully in her jeans. *She looks like a woman, and I look like a ten-year-old,* he thought. Darrell knew there was no way a girl like her would ever be his girlfriend.

"So, Darrell, how was your first day at Bluford?" she asked warmly. "I've been here forever, and I had a miserable day. I got two teachers mad at me because I forgot something I was supposed to turn in today. I dropped spaghetti on my shirt at lunchtime, and this guy I like dissed me for this other girl. But that's my problem. So how about you?"

Darrell was amazed at how friendly she was after ignoring him all day. It made sense, though, he thought. Around her friends, she was embarrassed to admit she knew him. But now that no one was around, she could act nice to him again. That's just the way things were if you were not popular.

"My day was . . . " Darrell paused. He was going to say what he usually said—"okay"—but then he stopped himself. "Bad. It was *really* bad. It was ten times worse than I thought it would be. I hate that school so much, I am about to walk back to Philly right now," he said.

"Really?" she replied, seeming shocked. "You must have some bad teachers. Mitchell is good, though. Who do you have for—"

"It's not the teachers," he said sharply. "They're all fine."

"Then what's the matter?" she asked.

"The kids. I hate them," Darrell said bluntly. "There's this guy, Tyray Hobbs, and he wants to kill me. And the rest of the school treats me like I'm invisible—"

"Darrell, you just got here! Give it a chance," Amberlynn said. "I mean you made one friend already."

"Who?" Darrell asked.

"Me, dummy!" Amberlynn laughed. "Gotta go. See you tomorrow."

Darrell watched her go up a side street. She had a blue and gold warm-up jacket with the words *Bluford Cheerleaders* on the back. He could hardly take his eyes off her. "Yeah, right," he muttered to himself. She could not even look at him during school, so how would she ever be his friend?

When Darrell arrived home, he was hungry—he had eaten very little of his lunch. He could not find anything in the refrigerator, so he decided to have a bowl of the ice cream his mother had him buy at the supermarket. That was the one good thing about being skinny, Darrell thought. He could eat whatever he wanted and never get fat.

As he scooped the ice cream into his bowl, he heard a funny sound outside the door. It sounded like crying, a cat maybe. Darrell listened more intently.

It was a kid crying.

Darrell opened the door and saw his cousin Nate sitting on the back steps sobbing.

"What's wrong, Nate?" he asked. The boy shrugged his shoulders. Darrell noticed Nate was holding something tightly in his hand. "Whatcha got there?"

"Nothin'," Nate said, sniffling and wiping his eyes. Pieces of what he was clutching dropped to the ground. Darrell could see small wheels and the red hood of a tiny race car.

"What happened to your car?" Darrell asked.

"My brother broke it!" Nate sobbed. "He broke my favorite car! I *hate* him!"

"Why'd he do that?"

"He did it 'cause he knew it was my favorite," Nate said.

"Go tell your mom and dad," Darrell insisted. He felt anger surging inside him just thinking about what Travis did.

"I can't tell on him," Nate said, picking up the pieces of his car. "He'll get worse if I tell on him. He always does." A tear rolled down Nate's face. He grabbed the last piece of the broken car and silently went inside.

Darrell knew how Nate felt. His little cousin was in the same situation he was in. Shaking his head, Darrell returned to his kitchen. "It shouldn't be this way," he said out loud. He wanted to stop what was happening to Nate and to himself. Darrell knew that this was just the way things were for people like him and Nate. But he was sick of it. And he was angry.

He went into his bedroom and looked in the mirror. Staring back at him was a short, skinny, scared kid. He took off his shirt and flexed his arms like the body-builders he had seen on TV.

There was not one ripple of muscle on his body. He was so skinny, he could see the ridges along his sides where his ribs were. "Oh, man," he groaned in frustration. Then he remembered what Mr. Dooling said about sports, about how they help build strength and confidence.

"Yeah, but Mr. Dooling never looked like me," he mumbled as he looked at his thin shoulders. No team would ever take him. Then he remembered what Malik always said to do—push-ups. Back home, Darrell had done them every once in a while, but he never did them regularly. Yet now things were different, he thought. Back home he had friends. Now he had kids laughing at him, and Tyray was after him. *I gotta do something,* Darrell thought. He was desperate. He was tired of being laughed at.

Darrell got on his hands and toes and did a push-up. And another. He kept doing them until his chest trembled and his arms burned. Then he heard his mother come home. He got up and looked in the mirror again.

Darrell glared at his naked chest. It did not look any different. He yanked a clean T-shirt out of a drawer and put it on. Nothing he did would matter, he thought bitterly. Like Nate, he was trapped. At least his cousin would grow up one day to be a big kid. But not Darrell. He would never be big. He promised himself he would do more push-ups tomorrow. Just then, his mother walked into his room.

"How was school, baby?" she asked.

"It was fine, Mom," he replied. He did not want to admit to her that he spent his entire first day alone. That would only add to her worries.

"I picked up some Chinese food from this restaurant near the office," she said. "Let's eat, and you can tell me all about what happened today." He followed her into the kitchen. She had ordered his favorite, sweet and sour chicken.

"I remember my first day of high school," she recalled as they sat down to eat. "I couldn't stop talking about it. I talked so much to your grandma that she fell asleep listening to me! So tell me about your day."

"Oh, not much happened, Mom. The teachers are okay. Mr. Mitchell, he teaches English. He's cool," Darrell said.

"Did you find someone nice to have lunch with? I know it's hard to find people to eat with when you're new, and it feels awful to eat alone," she said with concern.

"Yeah, I found somebody," Darrell said.

"Who?"

"Oh, some guy from my English class. He's pretty nice."

"See?" Mom replied, smiling. "Didn't I tell you you'd find a nice friend? And you were so worried. I told you things would be all right."

"Yeah," Darrell mumbled. He used to tell his mother everything that happened at school, but he stopped doing that when things got embarrassing. He liked having her think everything was okay, although it made him feel even more alone. *At least one person doesn't think I'm pathetic,* he thought. Even back in Philadelphia, he did not tell her the truth about all the times Malik fought his battles.

"My day was pretty good too," Mom said, smiling. "Everybody was friendly and helpful. I feel like I already fit in, and it's only my first day."

"That's good, Mom." He was glad she did not have a day like his, but he felt even more miserable because his mother had such an easy time on her first day. *What's wrong with me?* he thought. He wished she would hate California and decide to move back to Philadelphia tomorrow. Or better yet, right now.

Darrell finished dinner, cleaned the dishes, went to his room, and closed the door. He did a few more push-ups, but his arms were tired. His mother must have noticed that he was not being himself because she came into his room a few minutes later.

"Are you sure you're okay, Darrell?" she asked. "I know this move isn't easy for you."

"Mom, I'm fine."

"Well, if you need to talk about something, you don't have to talk to me. You can always go to Uncle Jason," she said.

There's no way I would ever speak to that man about anything, Darrell thought. "I know, Mom."

"Jason is another reason I moved us here. I think it is good to have a man around, and Jason has always wanted to be closer to you. Besides, he seems so good with his sons, I thought having him around might make it easier . . . especially if you ever wanted to talk to a man about man stuff."

Darrell felt sick. Every time his uncle looked at him, Darrell could tell he was sizing him up, judging him. Even worse, Darrell knew he did not measure up in his uncle's eyes. And he knew Uncle Jason had no idea what was happening with his own boys. He was so busy teaching them to be tough that he did not notice one of them was getting hurt. He taught Travis that strength was a way to force others to do what you want, and he taught Nate that strength meant not telling others when you needed help. Both sounded like bad lessons to Darrell. *I don't need that man's help,* he thought. *And I don't want it.*

"Thanks, Mom," he said. "Maybe I'll talk to him."

"Good," she sighed, looking relieved.

"Now, can you do me a favor? I've got this coupon for oranges at the super-market, and it expires today. Do you think you could run down there and pick up a bag? I'd go, but my feet are tired."

"Sure, Mom," Darrell said. *Lugging ten pounds of oranges might help build muscles,* he thought. He grabbed the coupon and some money and headed out the door. The street was pretty empty. It was a good time to head to the store because most people were inside eating dinner. *An hour or two from now,* Darrell thought, *the older kids will be hanging out in the streets. Some will be looking for trouble.*

But not yet, he hoped. A nervous chill ran down Darrell's back as he hurried down the street.

The supermarket was much different than when he met Amberlynn. The lines were short, and it took him only a few minutes to make his purchase. Hoisting the bag on his shoulder, Darrell left the store and headed home. He had walked about a block when he saw three kids jogging across the street towards him. As they got closer, he realized the one in the middle was Tyray. Darrell's stomach sank, and his chest started to pound. He wanted to drop the oranges right there and sprint home.

"Hey, Darrell Mercer," Tyray said as they stepped onto the curb.

Darrell kept walking. He hoped if he got close enough to home, they'd leave him alone.

But Tyray and his friends moved in front of Darrell and stopped, blocking his path. "I'm talking to you, fool," Tyray said, jabbing his index finger into Darrell's forehead, snapping his head back. "Don't act like you don't hear me!"

"I'm in a hurry. I gotta get home," Darrell mumbled.

"Hear that?" Tyray glanced over to his friends. "The boy says he's in a hurry. He's gotta get home to his momma," Tyray said in a mocking tone. "Man, you ain't nothin' but a little punk." Tyray spat as he spoke. Droplets of spit landed on Darrell's cheek. He was so scared he could barely talk.

"Please, man. I gotta go home," Darrell said, almost whimpering.

"I think poor Darrell's going to cry," Tyray replied, putting his hands to his own eyes, pretending to wipe away tears. His friends chuckled. Then Tyray sniffled as if he were crying. "Mom, I hate the kids in this neighborhood," he said, bending his knees so he was as short as Darrell. "Everybody picks on me, Mommy." Tyray's voice became high-pitched, as if he were imitating a young child. Then he heaved his chest and made several loud sobbing noises. Even his face twisted into a false display of sadness and hurt. Tyray's friends laughed so hard they could barely stand.

Rage boiled within Darrell, so much so that tears welled in his eyes, making him look as if he really was crying. He hated being this scared. He hated himself for being so small and weak that he could be humiliated just a few blocks from his own house. And he hated Tyray with every cell in his body. But he felt that if he even tried to hit Tyray, he would be beaten to a bloody pulp, that he might never make it home.

Then Tyray shoved Darrell into one of his friends. That kid shoved him back.

Tyray yanked Darrell by his shirt and brought his face so close that the two were staring directly into each other's eyes. Another boy grabbed Darrell's arms and held them behind his back. "How much cash you got on you, boy?"

Tyray asked. "Me and my boys got plans for this evening, and we need some money," he added, his voice suddenly becoming serious.

"I got no money on me," Darrell said. "I spent it all on these oranges."

Tyray whipped out a knife and held it up to Darrell's face.

Oh no, Darrell thought, *he's gonna kill me. This is the end. I've been in California for three days, and I am gonna die right here on the street.* He imagined how his mother would have Thanksgiving dinner in two weeks without him, and how sad she would be. He cringed and waited for the knife to rip into his body.

Tyray stabbed the orange bag, cutting a wide hole in it with the tip of his knife. Oranges dropped out and went rolling in all directions. Then Tyray shoved Darrell to the ground. As he struggled back to his feet, Tyray's friends began stomping on the oranges, crushing them into a juicy mush on the sidewalk. When Darrell saw what they were doing, he rushed to get to the fruit before the boys did. But they outnumbered him. It quickly became a game for them, stepping on the oranges before Darrell could pick them up.

The frantic struggle ended when Tyray grabbed Darrell's shirt and pushed him against a parked car. Darrell was trapped.

"Next time you better have cash for me, hear? Tomorrow morning, I'll be waiting right in front of the supermarket. You better be there," Tyray said. He crushed one more orange and then went back across the street. His friends followed him.

Darrell dried the tears from his eyes. He had never been more frightened in his entire life.

Chapter 6

After Tyray and his friends left, Darrell sat alone on the sidewalk. His whole body was shaking.

When the boys were out of sight, he started gathering the oranges that were not ruined. Though the bag had been slashed, Darrell had no choice but to use it to carry the remaining oranges home. Each time he took a step, an orange would slip out through the hole. He was bending to pick up an orange that had rolled into the street when he heard someone behind him.

"Here's an extra bag, honey," said a heavy-set woman holding two bags. She was emptying one by moving a few groceries to the other. "That bag of yours ain't good for nothin'."

"Thank you," said Darrell, gratefully taking the bag. He started packing oranges into it.

"You're welcome, child," the woman said. "I don't believe I've seen you around here before."

"I just moved here from Philadelphia. I live a few blocks up the street. My name is Darrell," he told her as he put the last orange into the bag. Darrell was glad to find that most of the fruit was intact. Only six oranges were too crushed to keep.

"Well, I'm Mrs. Davis. I live in that apartment house at the corner. Just me and my grandson Harold. I'm raisin' him all by myself," she said, pausing. She seemed lost in thought for a second. Then she asked, "Say, you wouldn't be goin' to Bluford, would you?"

"Yeah, I'm a freshman there," Darrell said.

"Well, praise the Lord!" Mrs. Davis cheered. "The good Lord musta intended us to meet 'cause my grandson, Harold, he's a freshman too. That poor child is having a tough time in high school because he's so shy. He needs some friends to talk to. You seem like a nice boy. Would you look for Harold in school and try to make friends with him? I'd be so grateful."

"Yeah, I can do that," Darrell said. He knew who Harold was. He was the guy who seemed to nod at him during algebra. Now Darrell knew why the boy had not spoken to him. Harold was shy.

"You know, Darrell, Harold's life ain't always been easy. Sometimes he's so quiet, it's like he's crawled into a shell. And, oh, how I worry. Just look for him sittin' by himself in a corner somewhere," Mrs. Davis said.

Darrell noticed that her description described him as much as it did Harold. "I'll find him, Mrs. Davis," Darrell promised. "And thanks for helping me."

"Wasn't any trouble at all," she said. "Oh, one more thing, child. Don't let Harold know I talked to you. He would feel bad about that. Just act like you ran into him by accident."

"Okay," Darrell agreed.

A big smile spread across the woman's wide face. Then she turned around and walked towards her apartment on the corner.

Darrell hoisted the bag of oranges onto his shoulder and went home. It seemed like days had passed since he left to go to the supermarket, but the living room clock indicated that only an hour had gone by. Exhausted, Darrell put the fruit in the kitchen, went to his bedroom, and closed the door. He never wanted to go outside again, let alone go back to school tomorrow.

Darrell flopped on his bed and stared at the ceiling. *What am I going to do about Tyray?* he wondered. Even if he dodged him tomorrow morning by taking the back way to school, he would run into Tyray eventually. He felt trapped. He and his mother could not afford to give money to Tyray every day, but if he did not, he knew he would suffer. He had to do something, but what?

If only I were bigger and stronger, Darrell thought. *Then Tyray would leave me alone.* But how could he make himself stronger? Darrell thought about Mr. Dooling's words—*"Sports help you build strength and confidence."* Still, he could not picture himself playing basketball or running track. He could not see himself wrestling either. Darrell remembered what the kid in his gym class had said. If Darrell joined the wrestling team, he would be the practice dummy.

Darrell thought about Tyray again. In his mind, he replayed all that had happened after dinner. Again, he felt Tyray's spit landing on his cheek and smelled his stinking breath. Again, he saw Tyray's face mocking him. But the worst was the laughter. Alone in his quiet room, Darrell could still hear Tyray and his friends laughing. Enraged, he slammed his fist into his pillow.

Then Darrell dropped to the floor and began doing push-ups. When he finally went to bed, his arms felt like rubber bands. That night, he dreamt he was trapped on the street again with Tyray and his friends. They were stomping and crushing round objects on the ground just as they had a few hours earlier. Only in this dream, the objects were not oranges. They were tiny human heads. And each one had a face—Darrell's face.

The next morning, Darrell jogged to school using back streets to avoid Tyray. At one point, he thought he saw Tyray and Rodney in the distance, but Darrell moved so quickly, they did not seem to notice him. When Darrell neared Bluford, he blended into a large crowd of students moving towards the school. Once inside, he hurried to his locker and rushed to class. He did not want to be caught in the hallway.

Darrell was relieved when he made it to English class and Tyray and Rodney were not there. But the two boys arrived several minutes later. Tyray scowled at Darrell as he came into the classroom. Darrell pretended not to see him. Though Mr. Mitchell was at the chalkboard when they entered, Tyray still managed to elbow Darrell as he walked by his desk. The teacher did not seem to notice.

After class started, Tyray glared back at Darrell a few times. Once he even made a fist and punched into his palm, making a slapping sound. Darrell tried his best to ignore him, but he was scared. Halfway through the class, Mr. Mitchell noticed what Tyray was doing.

"Mr. Hobbs," Mr. Mitchell said, "to do well in this class, you need to pay attention to what's happening in the front of the room—not the back." Tyray turned around and left Darrell alone for the rest of class.

At lunchtime, remembering his promise to Mrs. Davis, Darrell decided to look for Harold. After buying a slimy brown slab of meatloaf, he scanned the cafeteria. In a far corner, he noticed a boy hunched over a plastic tray, eating alone. It was Harold.

Darrell was happy to see the lonely boy. Without him, he too would have to endure another lunch alone. Now at least he could walk knowing where he was going. As he approached the table, he hoped Harold would like him.

"Anybody sitting here?" Darrell asked.

Harold glanced up in surprise. "No . . . sit down."

Darrell pulled up a chair and sat across from Harold. *Finally,* he thought, *I am not alone.* He looked over at Harold. The boy was taller than Darrell, but slightly overweight. He had his grandmother's soft round face. Harold did not look at him. He seemed afraid to make eye contact.

"My name is Darrell Mercer," Darrell said.

"I'm Harold," the boy said nervously, "Harold Davis."

Darrell wanted to talk to Harold, but he could not think of anything to say. Then he looked at his lunch. "Man, what is this stuff?" he asked, picking up a hunk of the soggy meat. "It looks like a piece of my shoe."

Harold smiled. "Your shoe probably tastes better than this," he said, flicking a chunk of meat into a white glob of mashed potatoes.

Both boys laughed. At first it was nervous laughter, but then it grew more relaxed. They started talking about the school and the teachers they had. After lunch, they walked together to their next class, algebra.

In class, Darrell saw Amberlynn again. This time she smiled and said "hi" to him. *Things are definitely better today than they were yesterday,* Darrell thought. But he still had to get through gym. As the time for the class drew closer, Darrell could feel knots in his stomach. By the time the bell rang, his hands were trembling.

Darrell went to the locker room as quickly as possible. He wanted to get changed before everyone else arrived. As soon as he changed, he headed into the gymnasium to wait for Mr. Dooling.

This is it, Darrell thought. *This is where Tyray is going to get me for not meeting him this morning.*

Tyray and Rodney came out of the locker room a few minutes later. Mr. Dooling had not come out yet. "There's the little punk that didn't show up this morning. You better have somethin' for me, or those oranges ain't going to be the only things that get crushed." Tyray's voice was loud, and other students turned to watch what was happening.

"I told you last night, I ain't got no money," Darrell replied. Just then Mr. Dooling arrived with his attendance sheet. Tyray quickly moved away.

"Today, we're continuing your conditioning. We'll jog like yesterday. Only now we're adding one extra lap around the track," Mr. Dooling said.

Many students groaned.

"Don't worry. It's not a race. I want everyone to run at a good steady pace. Let's go."

Again, the class headed outside and started jogging. Within a few minutes, the crowd of runners spread out. Like the day before, Darrell watched over his shoulder as Tyray and Rodney closed in on him.

"Look at those legs, man. That boy runs like a chicken," Rodney said, getting nearer.

"That boy *is* a chicken," Tyray said.

The two boys jogged right up behind him. Darrell tried to ignore them. Again, he figured as long as he stayed near Mr. Dooling, he would be safe. But as the class began the second lap, Darrell noticed Mr. Dooling had stopped. He was talking to another gym teacher who was also outside with her class. Darrell did not know what to do. He decided to run faster.

"Look at the midget go," Tyray said. "You better keep runnin', boy, 'cause if you stop, you might not run again for a long time."

Darrell sprinted as fast as he could. The three boys had moved towards the front of the pack of runners, but Darrell could not keep the pace. He knew he was not as fast as Tyray or Rodney. He was already out of breath, and his heart was pounding. Darrell looked over his shoulder and saw Mr. Dooling in the distance, gradually beginning to catch up. He still did not know what to do. Then he felt a sharp kick against his ankle. The blow knocked Darrell's feet out from under him. He flailed his arms out and fought to catch his balance, but Tyray kicked at his legs again. This time, Darrell tumbled to the ground, scraping his knees against the rough track surface. Other kids jumped to avoid stepping on him. A few laughed as they passed.

"That boy is clumsy!" Tyray said, as he ran away.

Darrell wanted to scream, *Tyray did it! Tyray Hobbs kicked me!* when Mr. Dooling caught up to him. But he only gritted his teeth and rubbed his ankle. He knew not to tell on Tyray. That would only make his torment even worse.

"Take a rest, Mercer," Mr. Dooling said as he jogged by. "Pace yourself better next time. I told you this is not a race."

By the time Darrell was ready to begin running again, the class was heading back to the locker rooms. Some went right to the showers. Others changed quickly and waited for the final bell to ring so they could go home. Darrell was worried. He was one of the few people who had not changed back into his clothes. He knew he stood out more than ever. Quickly he hurried to his locker. Just as he opened the metal door, a large hand reached over his shoulder and yanked his clothes out. Darrell knew it was Tyray. Rodney was standing on the other side of him, blocking anyone else's view of what was happening.

"Give me my clothes!" Darrell exclaimed.

"Fool, those are mine," Tyray shouted.

"What are you doin'? You some kinda thief or something?" he asked. Then he and Rodney moved into the crowd waiting by the door. Darrell knew that other kids had seen what had happened, but none were willing to stick up for him.

"Those are *my* clothes," Darrell said, following behind Tyray. Many of the kids standing by the door turned to look at Darrell. A few started laughing and making snorting noises. Tyray managed to squeeze himself into the front of the crowd nearest the door. Darrell could see his clothes under Tyray's arm. Then the bell rang. Within minutes, the entire locker room cleared out, and Darrell found himself completely alone. The only clothes he had were the T-shirt and shorts he was wearing.

I don't want to walk home this way, Darrell thought. He knew he would end up passing Tyray and his friends on the way home from school and they would laugh as soon as they saw him.

Darrell sat down on a bench in front of his locker. He wanted to wait until the hallways were empty so fewer people would see him in his gym clothes. Just then, he heard a door open, and Mr. Dooling walked in.

"What's the matter with you, Mercer?" Mr. Dooling asked. "Why aren't you dressed?"

Darrell hesitated for a minute. He was too embarrassed to admit the truth. "I guess somebody picked up my clothes by mistake," he said. "I can't find them."

Mr. Dooling shook his head. "Well, you can't stay here. See if you can find something to wear in this basket. Then get going," he said, handing him a basket filled with musty clothes that students had left in the locker room and never claimed.

Darrell rummaged through the basket and found a pair of jeans that fit him. After changing, he went to his locker, picked up the books he needed, and headed out of the school. In a dumpster along the side of the building, he saw his clothes. They were covered with orange peels and ice-cream-sandwich wrappers.

Darrell felt as if his head would explode. He could not take this anymore. He wanted to scream. Instead, he yanked his dirty clothes out of the dumpster and walked home.

Darrell was grateful his mother was not home when he got there. It gave him time to dump his dirty clothes into the washer without her asking questions. Then he went to his room, hid the jeans he took from gym under his bed, and did more push-ups.

I can't keep running from Tyray, Darrell thought. He knew that Tyray would corner him sooner or later, and he knew the next time would be worse. The only solution he could think of was to give Tyray his lunch money. *I don't want to give him Mom's money,* he thought. *But what choice do I have?* Darrell figured out how much money he could spare. If he did not buy any drinks at lunch, he could give Tyray fifty cents a day. *Would that be enough to stop him?*

That evening when his mother came home, Darrell pretended to be doing homework. He could not face her knowing that he was going to give her hard-earned dollars to a kid he hated. He did not want her to know what a weak, frightened boy her son was.

The next morning, Darrell walked on the main street to Bluford. He knew Tyray would confront him, but at least it would happen when he expected it. Although he hated the idea of giving Tyray money, he was tired of being terrorized in school, and he just wanted to put an end to it as soon as possible. Darrell was not surprised when he spotted Tyray and his friends standing near the supermarket.

"Look who it is," Rodney said, watching Darrell approach.

"There's the punk who's been hiding from me," Tyray said. "Boy, you better have some money for me 'cause I've lost all my patience with you." He walked over to Darrell and stared down into his face. "Whatcha got, fool?" he asked.

"Me and my mom don't have much money," Darrell whimpered. "I can give you fifty cents a day."

"Fifty cents?!" Rodney and Tyray laughed. Darrell cringed.

"Boy, you are going to have to do better than that! I can't even buy a soda on that. You give me the two dollars you pay for lunch every day, you hear? That's cheap enough for you and your poor momma," Tyray said, pushing his chest against Darrell's.

Darrell fumed inside. No one had the right to call his mother poor, even if it was true.

"But I won't be able to eat lunch," Darrell said. "I need money to eat."

"Boy, if you mess with me, you won't have teeth left to eat anything!" Tyray yelled, grabbing Darrell by the top of his shirt. "Now listen up. You meet me here every Friday morning. You give me ten dollars, and Rodney and me will be a little nicer to you. If you forget to pay one time, I'll bust you in half. If you tell anyone about this, I'll put your skinny butt in a cast. You got that?"

Darrell nodded.

"I'll see you here on Friday, Darrell Mercer. You and my money," Tyray said with a smirk. Then he and Rodney slapped hands and started laughing.

Darrell went on to school. He never felt worse about himself. He had always been picked on. But never in his life did he pay someone to leave him alone. Darrell wondered what Malik would say if he knew what he was doing.

In English, Tyray went to his desk in the front of the room without bothering Darrell. Only once did he look back. This time, instead of threatening Darrell, Tyray rubbed his fingers together as if he were holding money. Then he mouthed the word "Friday" without making a sound. Darrell knew what he meant. Tyray was warning him not to forget.

"Tyray and Darrell, do you two have something to share with this class?" Mr. Mitchell asked suddenly, surprising Darrell.

Darrell shook his head.

"I don't think Darrell should have to share with anyone. Just look at how little he is. He needs to keep everything for himself," Tyray said, acting sincere and innocent. The class chuckled at his comment. Darrell wanted to hide under his desk. He just sat there motionless.

"Tyray, if you have any other helpful comments, you are welcome to share them with me after school today," Mr. Mitchell said dryly.

"Sorry, sir," Tyray said, turning around to face the chalkboard.

After class, as Darrell gathered his books, Mr. Mitchell approached him.

"Darrell, is everything all right? You seem like you have a lot on your mind."

"I'm still getting used to it here. It's a lot different from Philly," Darrell said.

"Look, Darrell, I know what it's like to be new in a high school. It's not easy. If you ever need someone to talk to, I'm right here. You know where you can find me."

"Thanks," Darrell replied mechanically.

Darrell knew Mr. Mitchell was trying to help, but he could not bring himself to talk to the teacher. Back home, Darrell and his friends made it a rule never to bring adults into their problems, especially teachers. Now, Darrell wasn't so sure.

"Thanks again," he said as he left Mr. Mitchell's classroom.

On Friday morning, Darrell headed to the supermarket parking lot with ten dollars. The four-block walk from home felt like the longest walk he had ever taken. Each step required great effort, as if his feet were made of concrete. Even the money in his pockets felt uncomfortably heavy, and every muscle in his legs and back felt slow and achy. It was as if his body was quietly protesting what he was doing.

Darrell knew that paying Tyray was wrong. The shame and guilt he felt for giving his mother's money to a bully swept over him in unending waves. What kept him going was the hope that Tyray and Rodney would stop hurting him, that he would be able to walk through Bluford without feeling threatened.

A few minutes after he arrived at the supermarket parking lot, Darrell spotted Tyray and Rodney coming towards him. Tyray led the way. He was smoking a cigarette. Both boys eyed Darrell as they approached.

"Whatcha got for me, little man?" Tyray asked. He threw his cigarette down, walked directly in front of Darrell, and blew a cloud of smoke into his face.

The smoke stung Darrell's eyes and caused him to cough for a few seconds. Tyray smirked. Then Rodney mumbled something, and both boys chuckled. Quickly, Darrell reached into his pocket and pulled out six one-dollar bills and a handful of change. When they saw the change, Tyray and Rodney looked at each other and started laughing.

"That boy musta robbed his momma's piggy bank to pay us," Tyray said between fits of laughter. Darrell looked down in shame. Because he had spent some of his mother's money earlier in the week on lunch, he only had six dollars to give to Tyray. To make up for what he had spent, Darrell had taken money from his old change jar. He barely had enough coins to add up to the remaining four dollars.

Tyray took the money from his hands. "Darrell Mercer, you are the sorriest punk in all of Bluford. Ain't no one else there who's as small, dumb, and poor as you." The words were like sharp knives. Darrell knew they were true. He opened and closed his eyes to hold back tears. He could feel Tyray and Rodney looking at him, judging him.

"Mommy, the kids are being mean to me again. Nobody likes me here. I think I'm gonna cry," Tyray whined. His voice was high-pitched and raspy like the sound of screeching brakes on an old city bus. As he spoke, Tyray twisted his face into a look of mock sadness, and pretended to sob uncontrollably. Rodney howled in laughter. Then, both boys slapped hands and turned back towards Darrell. A crooked smirk spread across Tyray's face.

Darrell hated them. He hated the power they had over him. He hated that they knew what hurt him most. But more than anything else at this moment, Darrell hated the smirk on Tyray's face. It was vicious, ripping through Darrell as sharply as any insult. Through Tyray, Darrell saw how pathetic he was to the rest of the world. He saw something else too, something that frightened Darrell as much as it enraged him. In Tyray's gleaming eyes, Darrell saw the bully's pleasure in humiliating him. Tyray's smirk made Darrell want to crawl into a hole and never see another person again.

"Next time, I want dollar bills—not change. You hear me?" Tyray said, poking his finger forcefully into Darrell's chest. "Or else you'll be swallowing your own teeth," he threatened.

Darrell nodded. He could not look into Tyray's face. The shame hung on him like a weight tied to his chin, forcing his head down and his eyes to stare at the ground. Silently, Darrell turned around and walked towards Bluford. Behind him, he heard Tyray and Rodney resume their laughter. At one point Darrell thought he heard Rodney say "stupid fool." He did not turn back.

With each day that passed at Bluford, Darrell hoped things would get better, but they never changed. Every day, he lived with the fear of Tyray and the shame of paying him. The stress took its toll on his schoolwork. Darrell could not concentrate on anything, and his grades reflected it. Even in subjects he once got B's in, Darrell was now getting C's.

But grades were just part of his problem. In school, Darrell could not look into the eyes of his peers. He was sure most kids at Bluford knew he was giving away his mother's money, and he feared they would laugh at him just as Tyray did on Friday. He wondered if anyone else from Bluford was watching when Tyray grabbed the money from him and gloated. The second time Darrell paid him, Tyray forced him away with a violent shove. Darrell left the parking lot quickly, hoping no one would see him, but he was sure someone did. And they must have told the rest of the school. *Girls must know what I'm doing,* he said to himself. *That's why they won't even look at me.*

The only girl at Bluford who Darrell had really talked to was Amberlynn, but even she seemed to speak to him less. *She must know too,* he thought. He figured she did not want to talk to a coward. The only other person at Bluford Darrell really knew was Harold. But one day Harold was sick and missed school, and Darrell sat at lunch alone again. Darrell knew he had to do something, and he needed to do it soon.

At home, things were not much better. His mother, caught up in her new job, never questioned Darrell when he told her school was "fine." She did not seem to notice that Darrell was packing lunches either. He wondered if she noticed how quickly the peanut butter and jelly disappeared. One time she asked him if his appetite had increased. "Yeah, Mom," he said, "I'm hungry all the time." He could not tell her the truth—that he was bringing lunch to school and saving her money for his Friday payment to the bully.

"You know what it means when your appetite increases, Darrell?" she asked. "It means you are getting your growth spurt. Soon you'll look like your Uncle Jason." Darrell was glad she was happy, but he felt guilty allowing her to believe such a lie.

You have no idea what is happening to me, he thought as she smiled at him. But he said nothing. Darrell knew that now, more than ever, he was completely alone.

That is when he decided to take up Mr. Mitchell's offer. He knew the English teacher might have forgotten or not meant what he said, but Darrell did not know what else to do. The more he thought about Tyray and his own slipping grades, the more he realized he had to speak to someone.

On the last school day before Thanksgiving weekend, Darrell headed for Mr. Mitchell's classroom. Darrell had just left his last class and was moving quickly, eager to catch Mr. Mitchell before he left. He was grateful to find the teacher at his desk.

"Mr. Mitchell," Darrell said, "you got a minute?"

"Yeah, sure, Darrell," Mr. Mitchell said. "Have a seat."

Chapter 7

Darrell sat down in the chair closest to Mr. Mitchell. It was where Tyray sat. He did not know where to begin. As he searched for the right words, Mr. Mitchell broke the silence.

"You're having a rough time here, aren't you, Darrell?"

"Why do you say that?" Darrell asked, feeling defensive. He wondered if Mr. Mitchell was looking down at him the way kids at Bluford did. *Maybe Mr. Mitchell thinks I'm weak just like Uncle Jason does*, Darrell thought. Part of him wanted to get up and walk out of the classroom.

"Darrell," Mr. Mitchell said, "I was a lot like you when I was your age." Darrell looked closely at Mr. Mitchell. He was a stocky man with broad shoulders and dark skin. He was nearly six feet tall. He looked like he was never Darrell's size.

"Yeah, right," Darrell said. "You?"

"Really, Darrell. I was the smallest kid in my class, and big guys used to hassle me all the time. I got beat up at my bus stop once in front of a busload of kids. I even got my gym clothes put on a flag pole in front of the school. After all that, I started lifting weights and doing exercises, and it helped some. But what *really* helped was developing *inner toughness*," Mr. Mitchell said. "Now I know you're tough. Any kid who is picked on in school is putting up with a lot more than those who aren't picked on. Just coming to school knowing what your day is gonna be takes courage. I know. I've been there. What you got to remember is that you can always make yourself stronger. You can do it on the outside with sports and exercise. And you can also strengthen yourself on the inside, so you are tough enough to handle whatever happens."

"But how?" Darrell asked.

Mr. Mitchell looked through a few desk drawers and pulled out a book. "I have a book you should read," he said. "It's *Hatchet* by Gary Paulsen. It's a story about a boy stuck in a dangerous situation. To survive, he has to make himself stronger, both on the outside and on the inside. Read it. I think you'll get a lot out of it." He handed Darrell the book.

"Thanks," Darrell said. "But I don't like to read books." It was true. He could not remember the last time he finished a book.

"Darrell, you came in here looking for a change, right? Here is something that can help you get stronger. This isn't an assignment for class. But if you want my advice, read the book. I think it will help."

Darrell looked at the book. *How's this thing gonna help me with Tyray?* he wondered. The only way Darrell could see the book helping was if he hit Tyray over the head with it. Maybe Mr. Mitchell did not know what he was going through after all. Darrell put the book in his backpack. He was disappointed. He wanted an answer to his problem, not a book. He looked over at Mr. Mitchell.

"Darrell, if a student is really giving you trouble, I can help," the teacher said. "If he threatens you or hurts you, we can have him suspended or even expelled."

"No," Darrell replied. He knew that would just make it worse for him. "I want it to stop, but I want to be able to handle it myself."

"Well, if there comes a time when you really can't handle it, let me know, and I'll do what I can, okay? You're not alone," Mr. Mitchell said.

Darrell left the classroom feeling better now that someone knew how bad things were. But he still did not have a solution to his problem. Despite what Mr. Mitchell said, Darrell still was alone.

At home, Darrell raided the refrigerator, making himself two tuna fish sandwiches. He had gotten used to eating after school, especially since he started giving his lunch money to Tyray. *At least I don't have to see Bluford for four days*, he thought. The Thanksgiving holiday meant two extra days off from school.

After he finished his sandwiches, Darrell did push-ups. He had done them every day since he met Tyray. Once in a while, he thought that his arms and chest seemed a bit tighter than they used to be. But he still was shorter and skinnier than everyone in his class.

As he finished his push-ups, he thought about his conversation with Mr. Mitchell. *"But you can also toughen yourself on the inside,"* he had said. Darrell wanted to be tough all over, so tough he could look in the eyes of any kid that stared at him. He wanted to be so strong that no one would ever laugh when he was around. He wanted to be bigger, taller, and stronger than Tyray.

"Yeah, right," he mumbled. "I'll never be those things."

Still he wondered why Mr. Mitchell had insisted that he read a book. He went over to his backpack and pulled out *Hatchet*. *It's stupid to think a book can do anything about a bully,* Darrell thought as he opened it to the first page.

The book began with a kid named Brian going on a trip to visit his father. *So what,* Darrell thought. *I don't even have a father.* He turned the page. The story described how Brian had to take a private plane ride to get to his father's house. Darrell put the book down for a second. *Only a rich kid would be able to afford a private plane ride,* he thought. He did not feel like reading a book about a rich kid who had an easy life. Darrell wondered why Mr. Mitchell had given him the book. After reading two pages, he could not see anything good in the story. *I'll give it one more chance,* Darrell decided. Again, he picked it up and started reading. And then the book changed.

While Brian was flying in the small plane, the pilot had a massive heart attack and died right in front of him. Watching in horror, Brian realized he was stuck in a tiny plane high above a huge forest, and he did not know how to fly. Worse, Brian had to crash the plane in order to get back on the ground. Brian knew he might not survive the crash, but he had no choice. He had to land it. As Darrell read on, Brian was described as being totally alone.

Darrell may never have been in a plane before, but he knew what it was like to be in an impossible position. And he knew what it was like to be alone. He decided he would use the four days off to finish the book. He had nothing else to do. Besides, he wanted to see what was going to happen to Brian.

Thanksgiving weekend was the first time Darrell did not hate California. He did not mind it because he did not have to go outside. He did not have to go to Bluford or see Tyray. The only thing that bothered Darrell during the whole holiday was listening to Travis pick on his little brother. But even that was better than usual because Travis did not act as mean when his father was around. Darrell knew that hiding inside with his family for four days was not going to solve his problems, but it felt good to have time to relax.

On Thanksgiving Day, Darrell and his mother joined Uncle Jason's family for dinner. His mother had made a big honeyed ham, candied sweet potatoes, and creamed corn. His aunt and uncle had prepared a huge turkey along with a platter of stuffing cooked with butter. For dessert, there were apple, pumpkin, and cherry pies. Darrell made sure to eat everything. It seemed that when he ate, he only remained full for an hour or so. Then he felt hungry again. His mother teased him about his appetite, calling him "the bottomless pit." Uncle Jason seemed pleased that Darrell was eating so well.

"Maybe that boy will grow yet," he said to Darrell's mother. Darrell did notice that some of his clothes seemed tighter. But he still saw a scrawny guy staring at him in the mirror each morning.

"It doesn't matter how much I eat, I still look the same," he said to his reflection the day after Thanksgiving.

When he was not eating, Darrell was reading *Hatchet*. He could not put the book down. He eagerly read about how Brian managed to crash-land the plane in a small lake and how he narrowly escaped drowning. Then Brian faced new challenges. He had to find food, and after that, he had to protect himself from animal attacks. Darrell read the book late into the night, long after his mother went to bed. He still could not understand what it had to do with him or why Mr. Mitchell thought it was so important for him to read. But it didn't matter. Darrell liked the book. When he was reading it, he did not think at all about Tyray.

By the time Darrell finished the book on Saturday, he knew why Mr. Mitchell had given it to him. Brian was transformed in *Hatchet*. Changed completely. *Mr. Mitchell thinks I can change too,* Darrell thought. But how? It was the same question he had asked himself for years.

Darrell noticed that Brian was a lot like him. When Brian's plane crashed, he was severely bitten by insects and attacked by a porcupine that shoved its sharp needles deep into his leg. Then he got violently sick from eating poisoned berries. After each problem, Brian got angry and frustrated. He wanted to give up and go home. Darrell knew those feelings well. He wanted to give up every Friday and run back home to Philadelphia. Darrell may never have been alone in the woods, but he was alone at Bluford. And to him it seemed just as bad. Maybe worse.

But Brian changes in Hatchet, Darrell thought. *I'm never gonna change.*

Darrell read the part about Brian's transformation again. He wanted to see if there was a secret he was missing, a sentence that would give him the inner strength Mr. Mitchell had mentioned. If there was, he could not find it. In *Hatchet,* Brian changed when he realized that he was not going to survive alone in the woods. Darrell felt the same way about Bluford High School. He knew he had to change if he wanted to survive, but he did not know how. He hoped the book would give him answers, but all he had were more questions. He flipped through the pages again. Darrell noticed that Brian changed most when he started using his mind to solve his problems, instead of just complaining about them. At that point, he taught himself to build a fire, to fish, to make a shelter—to survive.

But real life is different, Darrell thought, *and I ain't Brian. I don't need to build fires. I gotta survive high school, not the woods.* Darrell would rather spend a night in the woods than another day at Bluford.

Though the book confused and frustrated him, Darrell had a favorite part. It was the end of the story, when a pilot came to rescue Brian. Instead of finding a scared kid, the pilot found a young man standing before him. Brian was still small, and he was exhausted. But he was strong, inside and out. And Brian was tough—tougher than ever because he had survived storms, injuries and wild animals. Darrell could feel his pulse quicken, imagining himself in Brian's shoes. *I want to be that tough,* he thought.

As good as the book was, Darrell still did not know what to do next. He still did not know how he would get friends, how he would learn to look people in the eye, or how he would deal with Tyray. He still felt like the same Darrell.

He wondered what Brian would do if he met Tyray.

Run back to the woods, he thought.

Chapter 8

On Monday, Darrell did not want to go to school. The next break would not be until Christmas, and all he could see was an endless string of miserable days stretching in front of him. Before he left, he grabbed the two peanut butter sandwiches he had hidden from his mother that morning and put them in his backpack.

During morning classes, Darrell could not concentrate on the day's lessons. He kept wondering if his life would change. But he also had another question, one he got from *Hatchet: What should I do to change things?*

Darrell was putting books into his locker just before lunch when someone shoved him from behind, sending his body halfway into the locker. The side of his head hit the metal door with a loud thud. Then he heard familiar laughter. It was Tyray and Rodney.

"Tyray, I told you to be more careful in the hallway. You might hurt somebody," Rodney said. Darrell looked up to see the two of them already halfway down the corridor.

Darrell wanted to yell. He had given them his mother's money, and they were still hurting him. Yet he knew if he said anything to either of them, his treatment would only get worse.

Darrell felt trapped again.

He glanced in his backpack. One of his sandwiches had been crushed when Tyray shoved him, and it leaked peanut butter into the inside of his bag. The smell of peanut butter was on everything. *Great,* he said to himself, *not only am I small and weak, but now I stink.*

He grabbed his backpack, slammed his locker shut, and rubbed the growing bump on his forehead. He knew other students in the hallway saw what happened. Some had even laughed with Tyray. Others just watched. Now as he looked around, everyone seemed to ignore him, acting as if nothing happened.

Quickly, Darrell slung his backpack on his shoulder and headed to the cafeteria to meet Harold. He was imagining Tyray and Rodney teasing him for smelling like peanut butter when he noticed a yellow piece of paper taped next to the cafeteria door. It read:

Build Confidence. Gain Strength.
Join the Bluford Wrestling Team.
No experience required.
Freshmen welcome.
See Coach Lewis for more information.

A picture of two guys wrestling was on the sign.

Those words again, he thought. *Confidence and strength.* His pulse quickened. Those two words were what he wanted. "But there is no way I can wrestle," he said aloud. Then he looked around to see if anyone had heard him. One girl with long braids stopped and looked at him as if he was crazy, then walked into the cafeteria. *I'm too small,* he thought. *People will laugh at me the second I step onto a wrestling mat.*

Then those words echoed in his mind again—*confidence and strength.*

But I am the weakest kid in this school, he thought.

Confidence and strength was the response.

Darrell was torn. He decided to talk about wrestling to Harold.

"Wrestling!" Harold exclaimed, when he told him about the sign. "Are you crazy? Have you ever seen a wrestling match? It's not the dumb stuff you see on TV with big guys who pull each other's hair. It's for real. That's the last sport I'd join if I were you. "

"Yeah, you're right," Darrell replied. He had felt the same way. But as he picked through his crushed peanut butter sandwich, Darrell thought about what Harold said. What had he meant by the words "if I were you"?

He meant that a skinny guy like me doesn't belong on the wrestling team, Darrell thought. He looked at Harold.

Harold silently put a spoonful of chocolate pudding into his mouth. As Darrell watched him, he realized something. Harold was scared too, maybe even more scared than he was. *And all he's gonna do is sit here at this lunch table hiding from everyone,* Darrell thought. He imagined the whole year ahead of him—maybe all four years of high school—passing like his first few weeks at Bluford. Darrell could not live like that. He could not live in fear. He did not want to. Darrell thought about *Hatchet* and how Brian realized the same thing and then forced himself to change. And he did it alone. *Maybe Harold isn't ready for a change*, Darrell thought, *but I am.*

"I gotta do something, Harold."

Harold looked at him and then looked quickly down at his tray.

"I'm gonna see Coach Lewis." Darrell said, getting up.

Darrell was nervous as he walked to Coach Lewis's office. Never had he imagined himself joining a wrestling team. As he was about to knock on the door, he considered turning around and heading back to the cafeteria. Then he thought of Brian and knocked.

"Come on in," said a deep voice from behind the door. Darrell walked in.

"Hi. I . . . I'm Darrell Mercer," Darrell stammered nervously. I'm here to see the coach . . . Coach Lewis."

"That's me, Darrell. How can I help you?" Coach Lewis was a muscular black man with cropped hair speckled with gray. The cinderblock walls of his office were covered with newspaper clippings, and a few trophies were in a case across from his desk.

"I saw the wrestling poster in the hallway. I wanted to know if I can join," Darrell said. He thought about how small he was and got embarrassed. He did not look the coach in the eye. "I'm new at Bluford, and I ain't ever wrestled before."

"Darrell, I don't care what you've done in the past. What I want to know is what you want to do now." Coach Lewis looked at him. Darrell felt like a little toddler in his gaze. "Wrestling is a tough sport. A lot of kids join up, but they quit after a few practices. That's a waste of time—theirs and mine." Darrell felt the coach may have been trying to tell him not to join.

Coach Lewis continued, "The real answer to your question, Darrell, will come from you, not me. I can teach any kid to wrestle as long as he is willing to work at it. I'm looking for kids who are gonna make a commitment. If you are one of those kids, I want you to come to practice with us. The choice is yours. Remember, the sport is like anything else in life. You've got to work hard to get good at it, and it takes time. But if you stick with it, you will grow. You'll grow inside and out, I promise you that," he said, smiling at Darrell.

"Does it matter that I'm so small?" Darrell asked. "I think I only weigh about a hundred pounds."

"Let's see what you weigh," Coach Lewis said. He walked Darrell over to a nearby scale. "One hundred and ten pounds," he said.

Darrell could not believe it. His mind started to spin. He had gained ten pounds since he had stood on a scale at the doctor's office in Philadelphia last summer, when he had to take a physical before enrolling in high school. The doctor had said he was in good health, but small. Now he was ten pounds bigger. *Ten pounds.* It was finally true, he thought—he was growing.

"Wrestling isn't like football or basketball. You don't need to be bigger to be better. Wrestling is sort of like boxing. You always go against an opponent who is the same weight as you. So it isn't size that makes you win. It is strength, endurance, and most of all, brains. So don't worry about your weight."

Darrell did not exactly feel relieved. He lacked strength and endurance just as much as he lacked size. As far as brains were concerned, Darrell could only guess that they were small too, especially when it came to wrestling. Coach Lewis seemed to sense Darrell's thoughts.

"Listen, Darrell. I have seen kids start wrestling in high school who were lighter than you. I've seen two of them become state champions. So quit worrying. It doesn't get you anywhere. If you want to accomplish something, you've gotta get to work." He handed a form to Darrell. "If you want to join the team, you've gotta fill this out and have your parent or guardian sign it. Get it to me tomorrow, and you can start practice then, okay? I hope to see you there, Darrell."

Darrell left Coach Lewis's office feeling different. He had not even filled out the form. But he still felt different. He knew he was going to join the wrestling team.

The next day, Darrell brought the form back completed and signed. His mother was happy to sign it, though she was barely awake when she scratched her name across the paper. Longer hours at work made her more exhausted in the evenings. When he took the sheet from her, she gave him a hug and told him she wanted to see his first match. "We'll see, Mom," he had said. He could not imagine himself wrestling.

At lunchtime, Darrell told Harold that he had decided to join the wrestling team. "Maybe I made a mistake, Harold, but I'm sick of feeling like a nobody. I'm thinking it might help, you know," he explained.

Harold shrugged. "I know how you feel, Darrell," he said sadly. "Let me know what happens. Maybe I'll join one day."

Just then Darrell noticed Amberlynn Bailey walk with Jamee Wills to a nearby table. Amberlynn wore jeans that rested snugly on her hips. "Man, don't she look good?" Darrell sighed. "That girl is *fine!*"

"You ever tell her you like her?" Harold asked.

"No! Are you crazy? I may be stupid, but I ain't *that* stupid. She don't want someone like me." Darrell shook his head. "For one thing, she's taller than me," he added.

Harold laughed between bites of his lunch, a cheeseburger with bacon.

"I did talk to her a few times. She's real nice . . . sometimes, anyway," Darrell continued, remembering the day she ignored him in class.

"Maybe she's different than other girls," Harold said. "Maybe she likes you."

"Yeah, right," Darrell replied bitterly. But inside his heart, a tiny flame of hope burned, one so small and frail that he was afraid to admit it even existed.

After his final class, Darrell went to his first wrestling practice. He was nervous as he put his books in his locker and made his way back to the gymnasium. He had never been at Bluford this late in the day.

As he rounded the corner and headed to the gym, he saw a group of cheerleaders walk by on their way to practice. Amberlynn was one of them. Darrell's heart fluttered as he watched her walk by in the blue and gold uniform. He noticed the graceful way she walked and the muscular shape of her calves as she moved down the hallway. She did not seem to notice him.

When Darrell got to the gym, he went straight to the locker room. It was much different this late in the day. The only people there were athletes. The guys changing out of their school clothes were bigger and more muscular than the average Bluford student. Surrounded by this group, Darrell stood out even more than usual.

"What are you here for?" said a kid

with a shaved head and the hint of a mustache. Darrell had seen the kid in the cafeteria, but he never spoke to him before.

"I'm going to wrestling practice," Darrell answered nervously. His voice scratched as he spoke.

"You! You're kidding, right?" the kid asked. "Look at you!"

Just then Coach Lewis came into the locker room. He looked over at Darrell and nodded with a smile.

"Okay, gentlemen. There are a few new people here today. I want you to welcome them and help them out as they get used to our system. For you older guys, I want you to remember what it was like when you first started. Be patient. For you new guys, this may be the hardest thing you've ever done. Work hard. Follow the older guys, and don't give up. Okay, everyone, get started."

When Coach Lewis finished talking, a group of about twenty guys headed out to the gymnasium. Darrell followed them. Immediately they went to one side of the huge room. In the corner were four thick ropes reaching from the floor to the ceiling of the gym. Quickly, the group broke into four lines, one by each rope. Darrell watched in horror as the line leaders climbed the ropes hand-over-hand without using their legs. *There's no way I can do this*, Darrell thought. *No way.*

As Darrell watched, he saw that not all the kids were able to go up using their arms. Some had to use their legs to help. Others barely reached the top. *They must be the new people,* he thought.

Then it was Darrell's turn. First he tried to climb with only his arms, but he could not hoist his weight. When he used his legs, he felt like a giant inch-worm climbing on a leaf. Yet for all his effort, he moved up only a few feet. Halfway up the rope, he was exhausted. Unable to hold on any longer, he let go and fell to the ground embarrassed. Instantly, another kid took his place on the rope and climbed to the top. Darrell shook his head and walked to the back of the line.

When everyone was done climbing, the group started to jog laps around the gym. Darrell was glad they were doing something he could do. Even though he was discouraged by the ropes, he still could not believe he was practicing with the wrestling team. Never in a million years would he have guessed that he would be doing such a thing. For a few minutes, he was almost proud of himself. Then the pace of the jog picked up, and he started to hurt.

The jog lasted about twenty minutes. Darrell was grateful when it ended. He was tired, sweaty and out of breath. He thought everyone would rest, but then he realized the group was moving over to the other side of the gym, where the wrestling mats were set up.

Darrell nervously stepped onto one of the huge blue and yellow mats. It smelled like rubber and felt soft and squishy, like a giant sponge. "Now we're going to start our workout," declared the team captain. A few people groaned. The word "start" echoed in Darrell's brain. What had he been doing if they were just starting now, he wondered.

For forty-five more minutes, the team exercised. They did push-ups, sit-ups, leg raises, jumping jacks, and a series of painful drills with names like "mountain climbers," "squat thrusts," and "lunges." Towards the end of the last drills, Darrell's arms and legs trembled, and his heart pounded. A few sharp cramps shot down the side of his stomach, making him want to double over. Yet he stayed with the group. Barely.

The next half hour of practice was wrestling drills. Darrell watched, learned, and practiced how to throw a standing person down in three different ways. He also learned how to avoid being thrown down if someone tried to use the takedowns on him. He was not skilled with the moves, but he got to know what they were. He liked learning the skills. It made him feel as if he had a secret weapon, one he could use if he ever needed it.

During the final half hour of practice, Darrell was assigned to wrestle with two other kids in his weight group. He was happy to see guys his size, even though they were much more muscular than he was. Coach Lewis explained that the three people in each group would take turns wrestling—two would wrestle while one rested. The matches were to last for one minute. One minute seemed short to Darrell, especially since they had been exercising for almost two hours already. Yet once he started actually wrestling, one minute seemed like an eternity.

In his first mini-match, Darrell wrestled a kid named Craig. In about fifteen seconds, Craig hoisted Darrell into the air and slammed his body down sideways into the mat. Darrell felt his face bounce off the mat's rubber surface. As Darrell struggled to get up, Craig jammed his forearm into Darrell's nose, hooked his arm, and pried him over onto his back. Darrell felt like a turtle turned upside down on its shell. Before he knew what was happening, Darrell's arms and legs were so tangled that he was unable to move. He could barely even breathe.

"You're pinned, Darrell," explained Coach Lewis. Craig let Darrell up. "That means you lose the match. Never roll onto your back," the coach added, and moved on to another group.

"Don't worry," said Craig. "You're still learning, that's all. Luis and I have wrestled for two years."

Sure, Darrell thought. *Why worry?* His back ached, his face was bruised, and he had lost in front of the head coach. *Everything is wonderful.*

In the next match, Darrell wrestled Luis. The result was nearly the same. Only this time, Darrell noticed, he was not pinned until just before the minute was over.

Maybe that's improvement, he thought.

Practice ended with a drill Coach Lewis called "steps," in which each member of the team carries someone of his weight or more up three flights of steps. Once a pair reached the top, they sprinted back to the bottom and switched places. Craig carried Darrell on his back up the entire length with ease. When it was Darrell's turn, each step was a struggle. His legs ached and wobbled. At one point, he thought he was going to collapse, sending himself and Craig tumbling down the steps. After he finally reached the top, Craig slapped him in the chest. "Good job," he said.

"Thanks," Darrell answered, managing a slight smile.

When practice finally ended, Darrell could barely walk. His day at Bluford was over three hours longer than it would have been if he had not gone to practice. He still had to walk the mile back to his house, and he still had homework to do. He had no idea wrestling would be so hard. By the time he got home, it was almost 7:00.

"How was your first practice, Darrell?" his mother asked when he walked in the door. "I was worried about you. You look exhausted."

"It was great, Mom," he mumbled, almost too tired to talk. He did notice that in addition to feeling tired, he also had an incredible, growling hunger. Slowly he trudged into the kitchen to the refrigerator. He devoured Thanksgiving leftovers as if he had not eaten in weeks, washing everything down with three glasses of cherry Kool-Aid.

"Honey, if you keep eating like that, you are really gonna grow," she said with a smile.

"I hope so, Mom. I really hope so."

After dinner, Darrell forced himself to do his algebra homework and then went to bed. He slept better than he had since the days before his mother told him they had to leave Philadelphia.

The next morning, Darrell could hardly move. Every joint in his body was stiff, and his ribs hurt whenever he inhaled. When he tried to stretch, hot knives of pain ripped into his back and sides. He could barely even raise his arms to brush his teeth. And once when he sneezed, he felt as if his whole upper body was going to shatter and fall to the floor like a broken window. He felt like he had aged fifty years in one night.

After packing his lunch, Darrell left

for school, making sure not to take the main street to Bluford.

Darrell arrived in English class a bit early, and Mr. Mitchell had not yet entered the classroom. When he sat in his seat, he noticed Amberlynn smiling at him. She was wearing black jeans and a snug white T-shirt. It seemed to him that it was the first time she noticed him in weeks.

"How's it goin', Darrell?" she asked in a friendly voice.

Darrell thought her voice sounded like music. For a second, he felt happy at Bluford. Finally someone talked to him, someone who was attractive and friendly. "Pretty good," he said, smiling back at her.

"Were you working out with the wrestling team yesterday?" she asked.

"Yeah. That was my first practice," he replied.

"Are you really going to be a wrestler, Darrell?" He was surprised at the look on her face and the excited sound of her voice.

He was not sure how to answer. Darrell could not imagine himself as a wrestler. The word just did not seem to fit him. He knew he was the weakest person on the team, and he wondered if he would be able to last through another practice, let alone the whole season. Still, he did not want to quit. Quitting would mean that nothing would change. He would be back where he started when he first set foot in Bluford. He shuddered as the images of Tyray and Rodney flashed in his mind. "I guess," Darrell said.

A wide smile spread across Amberlynn's face. "Well, Darrell, I love to watch guys wrestling. Maybe I'll see you at a match one day."

Darrell's heart fluttered. There was no way he would quit wrestling now. No way.

Just then, a group of students entered the classroom. Tyray and Rodney were among them. They stopped and glanced over at Darrell before moving to their seats. Darrell could tell that they noticed Mr. Mitchell's absence. Tyray whispered something to Rodney, and the two strolled slowly towards their desks like hawks circling their prey.

"Hey, Amberlynn. You got a new boyfriend? Are you sweatin' that midget from Philadelphia?" Tyray asked with a sneer as he pointed at Darrell. Nearly everyone in the class turned to watch what was happening. A few kids giggled, and Amberlynn turned away from Darrell. He could tell she was embarrassed.

Amberlynn's friend Jamee glared back at Tyray. "Why don't you shut up, Tyray? It's none of your business what Amberlynn does," she said.

"Hey, it must be true," Tyray said. "Amberlynn, you like this little punk? He may be small, but he's the biggest fool I know. Look at his sorry face. Can't you do better than that?!" Rodney and a few other kids cackled out loud.

Darrell wanted to disappear, to hide under his desk. He was embarrassed for himself, but he also felt guilty that he was causing embarrassment for Amberlynn. He wished for her sake that they'd never met.

"I don't like him or anyone right now," Amberlynn answered.

"I heard this punk joined the wrestling team. You know, Amberlynn, if you want to watch your little man wrestle, you're gonna have to go back to elementary school. He's gonna have to wrestle fourth graders 'cause he's so tiny."

Again, some students chuckled.

Darrell could understand why kids laughed at him, but he could not see why they laughed at Amberlynn. *What was so funny?* he wondered. Maybe the other kids went along with Tyray because they were afraid of him. That would make them all cowards, Darrell thought bitterly. At least he wasn't encouraging Tyray to hurt anyone. Everyone else who laughed along was.

"Tyray, leave me alone," Amberlynn yelled. "I don't have a boyfriend."

"Just shut your stupid mouth, Tyray," Jamee added.

"Uh oh, now you're sickin' your ugly friend Jamee on me," Tyray said. "Your wrestler boyfriend ain't man enough to stand up for himself, so you gotta send your girl after me. Man, she's almost as ugly as the little midget. She's more of a man than he is too," Tyray announced.

Then Rodney and about half of the class laughed even louder. Darrell squirmed in his seat. He did not want anyone to know that he had been paying Tyray to leave him alone. Then the whole class would think he was an even bigger fool than he seemed right now. He knew if he said anything, Tyray would jump all over him, showing no mercy. Darrell remained silent, hoping Mr. Mitchell would walk in. He wished he had never come to Bluford. He wanted to walk out of the high school and never return.

"He's not my boyfriend!" Amberlynn screamed. "I don't even like him! Do you hear me? I don't even like him!"

Tyray smiled, and he and the rest of the class looked at Darrell.

Darrell got up from his desk and left the room. Never in his life was he so humiliated. He fought hard to keep tears from rolling down his face as he walked out. He did not want anyone to see him cry, but he could not stop himself. He ran to the nearest bathroom, went into a stall, sat down on the dirty floor and sobbed. A few kids were hurrying out of the bathroom when he arrived, but none of them seemed to notice him. The first bell soon sounded, signaling the start of classes. Mr. Mitchell must have arrived by now, but Darrell did not want to go back to class. He never wanted to go to that room again.

He looked at his rumpled backpack on the floor, still open from when he was in English. Inside he saw his copy of *Hatchet.* Quickly he yanked it out of the bag and threw it out of the stall. He heard it strike the metal trash can across the room.

"I hate this place!" he said out loud, tears running down the side of his face.

But then Darrell started to think of *Hatchet.* First he worried about what Mr. Mitchell would say if he lost his book. Then he remembered why the teacher had given it to him in the first place. *To make me stronger on the inside,* Darrell thought. He walked out of the stall and picked up the book.

Carefully, he opened the cover and leafed through the pages. He stopped at the section where Brian was starving and his leg was full of sharp porcupine quills. For ten minutes, Darrell read over and over again how Brian cried about what had happened to him, but then realized self-pity would not solve his problems. Darrell flipped to the end scene and read his favorite part, when Brian survived and became a strong, confident young man.

Darrell realized he could not just give up. Like Brian, he hated what had happened, but crying in the bathroom didn't solve anything. Darrell knew he had to get back to class. He knew he would be ashamed to walk back into the room in the middle of the lesson, that all the kids would turn and stare at him. Yet he also knew he would be more ashamed if he never went back. Darrell wondered if Mr. Mitchell would punish him for being late. Since it would be the first time he was late, Darrell hoped Mr. Mitchell would give him a break.

He put the copy of *Hatchet* back into his backpack and walked down the hallway towards the classroom. He could feel his heart pounding as he approached the door.

I won't look at Amberlynn ever again, he thought. Then he walked in and sat down. Mr. Mitchell glanced at him as he entered the room, but then quickly resumed his lesson. The rest of the class stared at him for a second, and then went back to their work. The only person who did not look at him was Amberlynn Bailey.

Chapter 9

For three weeks, Darrell spoke to no one about what happened that morning in English class, not even Harold. Each day, he avoided Amberlynn. He did not want to embarrass her again. He was sure she wanted to stay away from him too—she always avoided looking at him. Though sad that he could not talk to her again, he understood and accepted it. *She needs to stay away from me,* he thought. *It's best for both of us.*

Since he joined the wrestling team, the days passed by in a blur. Each morning he got up and dragged himself to school. After classes, he forced himself to wrestling practice, and then he trudged home exhausted. At home, he would eat an enormous dinner, struggle to get through his homework, and then fall into a deep sleep.

The only thing that helped him mark the passing weeks was Tyray. Every Thursday, Tyray and Rodney warned him in gym class that he better be at the supermarket the next morning. And every Friday, Darrell would show up with his mother's money. Darrell hated the routine, but he was afraid of what Tyray would do if the money stopped coming.

The only time Darrell did not think about Tyray was at wrestling practice. As soon as he went into the locker room after school, it was as though he entered another world, a world Tyray could not enter. Practices remained tough, but as the weeks passed, Darrell was slowly getting stronger. After two weeks, he managed to get within a few feet of the gymnasium ceiling on the ropes. The warm-up runs also stopped bothering him. He even improved on the steps, gaining enough strength to carry Craig with more speed and control.

But his biggest improvement was in his wrestling skills. After two weeks of steady practice, Darrell had learned five takedown moves, and he was able to demonstrate them to Coach Lewis using Craig as his opponent. His favorite move, the double leg takedown, involved lifting his opponent completely off the ground and then slamming him into the mat.

Coach Lewis also taught the team three different ways to pin people. With each move he explained, the coach would also teach the "counter-move"— the way to get away if someone used the move against you.

Darrell learned quickly that wrestling was like chess. To master it, you had to use strategy. Craig and Luis had taught him this too. Though Darrell had never beaten either of them in practice, he had learned how to avoid being pinned, at least most of the time. He still lost constantly, but now it was because his opponents scored more points than he did. Each time they wrestled, Darrell watched what Craig or Luis did to defeat him, and slowly, he was becoming more of a challenge for them. Darrell hated losing in practice, but at least he was not being humiliated like he had been on the first day. Once, when Coach Lewis watched, Darrell escape being pinned by Craig. Coach yelled out, "Good job, Darrell! Never stop fighting, even if it looks like your opponent has you beat." He smiled and patted Darrell on the back. "You're gettin' there. You just gotta keep pushing. Next time, you try and pin *him.*"

Darrell hoped he would be ready for Bluford's first match against Lincoln High School in two weeks.

After practice one day, Darrell was changing back into his clothes when the kid with the shaved head walked by on his way to his locker. Darrell had learned from Luis that his name was Kevin and he was a junior at Bluford. Luis also told him that Kevin was one of the best wrestlers in the school and had gone to the city finals last year. When Kevin walked past him, Darrell pretended he did not notice. Then he heard a deep voice next to him. "Hey, Darrell." Darrell turned to face Kevin. He was about Tyray's size, maybe a little bigger.

"Yeah?" Darrell asked nervously.

"Good job today," Kevin said and walked out.

On Saturday after wrestling practice, Darrell ran into Jamee at the supermarket. He had gone to the store to buy more bread for his sandwiches. His mother still did not notice that he was making his own lunch each day. All she knew was that bread in her house seemed to disappear overnight. "You must be growin' now, baby," she said to him when she gave him the money for bread, "'cause I can't keep food in this house more than a day or two before it's gone."

When he saw Jamee, Darrell wanted to leave, but he was stuck in the middle of a long line with nowhere to go.

"Hey, Darrell," Jamee said as she walked over to him.

"Hi, Jamee. What's up?" he asked. Darrell had not ever said more than three words to her at any one time. *Jamee must think I am a fool, too,* he thought.

"Darrell, I just want you to know Amberlynn feels real bad about what happened in class that day with Tyray. She didn't mean anything she said. She was just actin' that way because everyone was starin' at her and she was embarrassed."

"Yeah, right," Darrell replied.

"Really, it's true. Amberlynn likes you. She told me she thought you were a really nice guy, and she doesn't like how things have been between you two. But she's afraid to talk to you 'cause she thinks you hate her because of what she did," Jamee insisted.

"She thinks *I* hate *her*? I thought *she* hated *me*."

"Listen, Darrell. Amberlynn thinks you're a nice guy, and if you'd talk to her, you'd find out. Then both of you can stop feeling bad about what happened. But if I were you, I wouldn't talk to her in class. I think Tyray kinda likes Amberlynn, and if he sees you talking to her, he's gonna start trouble all over again." Jamee rolled her eyes as she mentioned Tyray.

"So what am I supposed to do? Pretend I don't know her?" Darrell asked angrily.

"You gotta find a way to see her where you can talk." She paused for a minute. "Why don't you go to the Freshman Dance? It's the Friday before Christmas break. I'll make sure she's there." Just then Jamee glanced at her watch. "I have to go now to meet my sister. Just make sure you come to the dance," she instructed and walked out.

Watching Jamee leave, Darrell thought about what she said. Could it be true that Amberlynn really liked him? Part of him wondered if Jamee was lying. But another part of him was full of hope.

He had not been to a dance since eighth grade. Back then Malik, Reggie, and Mark were with him. They'd sit around and talk more than anything else. This dance would be different. Darrell would not have his old friends. But Amberlynn would be there. He pictured himself dancing with her, and his heart raced. He had to go to the dance. He just *had* to.

But what if Tyray came to the dance? Darrell knew he could not be seen with Amberlynn if Tyray showed up.

As he paid for the bread, Darrell wondered what he would do about the dance. He realized he still had a week to think about it, while his first wrestling match was less than a week away. For now, he would put the dance out of his mind.

The night before his first match, Darrell dreamed he was wrestling Tyray in front of a crowd of Bluford students. Tyray, with incredible speed, easily tossed Darrell around the mat and pinned him right in front of Amberlynn, who laughed loudly as he was pinned. Darrell woke up struggling to free himself from his blanket. He was relieved he had only been dreaming. But he dreaded the match to come.

Yet Darrell had been getting better in each practice. Three days before the match, he had managed to climb to the top of the ropes for the first time. Though still unable to beat Craig or Luis, he did manage to flip Luis onto his back for a second. Even Luis seemed surprised when it happened. Also, Darrell and Coach Lewis had recently discovered that Darrell was fast. Although he was not as strong as the other kids on the team, he was quicker. The coach told him speed could make him hard to beat. Darrell liked to think he had something other kids did not have. It was the first time he felt that his size was not hindering him.

What made Darrell even happier was his weight. All wrestlers had to weigh themselves before the match with Lincoln to make sure they were in the right weight group. When Darrell stepped on the scale, he discovered he had gained several pounds since he joined the team four weeks ago. He now weighed nearly 115 pounds. *Mom's right*, he thought when he looked at the scale. *I'm finally growing.* And there was no fat anywhere on his body.

The day of the match, Darrell walked in and out of classrooms like a zombie.

His mother promised him she would come to see him wrestle, and Darrell knew she would bring Uncle Jason. Besides them, dozens of Bluford students would be there watching him. Maybe even Amberlynn. He was so nervous that he could barely eat the sandwiches he had packed that morning.

At the end of his last class, Darrell walked to his locker and then to the gym to prepare for the match. One thought kept replaying itself in his mind: *I'm gonna lose.* Not only was he going to lose, he thought, but he was going to humiliate himself. As he changed into his blue and gold wrestling uniform, Darrell wanted to go home and crawl into his bed. He did not want to go out and wrestle. As he sat on the bench, he felt someone nudge his shoulder.

"You okay?" a voice said.

Darrell turned around to see Kevin looking at him.

"Nervous?" Kevin asked.

Darrell nodded.

"I remember my first match," Kevin said. "I was so scared I wanted to throw up. But as soon as I got started, I was fine. You'll be all right. Just remember one thing. It's your first match, so no one is going to expect you to be an expert. Good luck."

"Thanks," Darrell replied. It was good to hear Kevin's advice, but Darrell did not think he had anything in common with a champion wrestler.

It was time for the matches to begin. They were divided into three parts. First the inexperienced wrestlers from both high schools would have their matches. After that, the junior varsity and varsity teams would wrestle. Since Darrell was so light, his match would be among the first ones. Coach Lewis came over to talk to him just before his match.

"Listen, Darrell. You've come a long way in the past month. You work hard, and I'm impressed with your progress. Now, I know you're nervous. It's normal. The kid you're wrestling is as new and as nervous as you. Use your speed, and remember the moves we practiced, and you'll be fine. If he starts overpowering you, don't give up. Sometimes you can beat a stronger guy by just waiting for him to make a mistake. Just go out and do your best," Coach Lewis advised.

The coach slapped Darrell's back. Darrell slowly walked onto the mat. The Bluford crowd cheered as Darrell walked out. He could see his uncle and mother sitting next to each other in the bleachers.

"What am I doing?" Darrell mumbled to himself as he walked to the center of the mat. His opponent came out to meet him. The boy was slightly shorter than Darrell but a bit more muscular. Each boy put a foot on the starting marker. Darrell thought he was going to pass out.

"Come on, Darrell!" his mother cheered in the distance.

Then the whistle blew.

In a flash, the boy from Lincoln locked arms with Darrell. Alternately, each boy tried to throw the other to the mat. When Darrell tried to muscle his opponent aside, the boy barely budged. *He's much stronger than me*, Darrell thought. The boy tried to sweep in underneath Darrell to lift him up, but Darrell figured out what he was doing and escaped. Then Darrell tried his favorite move, the double-leg takedown. Quickly, he darted beneath the shorter boy, grabbed his legs and lifted him. The Bluford fans cheered as Darrell hoisted his opponent off the ground and rolled him into the mat. Darrell knew the move scored him two points. He was winning. Just then the whistle sounded. The first two-minute round was over. *Only two more rounds to go*, Darrell thought.

The referee waited for the boys to get in the starting position and blew the whistle. Instantly, the two wrestlers grappled with each other. Darrell struggled to find a way to flip his opponent onto his back, but the shorter boy's strength made it impossible for him to do anything. As Darrell fought to put the boy in a headlock, he escaped and flipped Darrell onto his side.

"That's one point for Lincoln," the referee said.

Before he knew what was happening, Darrell found himself crushed under his opponent, who was desperately trying to put him into a move of his own. Darrell rolled onto his stomach to avoid being flipped over.

"Don't get trapped, Darrell!" Coach Lewis yelled. The boy from Lincoln was fast. He wrapped his legs around Darrell in a move the coach called a "grapevine." The move took away Darrell's leverage so he had no way to stop himself from being rolled to his back. Each second they wrestled, the boy seemed to lock up another one of Darrell's limbs. Darrell felt himself being tilted over.

"Stay off your back!" Coach Lewis screamed.

Darrell was exhausted. His back was being wrenched and twisted. One of his arms was trapped, and his legs felt like they were chained to a wall. He flailed out his free arm, trying to get a hold of the mat to free himself, but it did not help. He felt like a bug squashed under a shoe.

This is it, Darrell thought. *This is where I lose in front of everyone.*

Then the whistle blew. The second round had ended. Darrell managed to avoid being pinned, but the boy from Lincoln had scored two points for nearly pinning him.

"Remember what I said, Darrell. Use your head! You can still win!" Coach Lewis instructed.

Darrell got back into the starting position for the final round. Again the whistle blew. Almost instantly the boy seized Darrell and tried to flip him. This time he used a move called the "cradle," one which Craig had often used against him. Darrell groaned as the boy's forehead jammed into his rib cage. He wanted to give up. If he just allowed the boy to pin him, it would all be over.

"Use your head, Darrell. You can beat him!" Coach Lewis screamed in the distance.

Everything seemed to pass in slow motion. Darrell could feel his opponent's arm wrapping under his leg. He felt the impact as the boy drove into his side, forcing him into the mat. He could almost see the whole match as it would appear from the stands.

"Come on, Darrell!" Coach Lewis screamed. To Darrell, he sounded like he was miles away.

Darrell raised his head and looked over at the stands. The Bluford side was filled with people yelling. Their voices blurred together so he could not understand what they were saying. He wondered if Amberlynn was out there watching him lose.

"Do something!"

The boy began tightening his hold on Darrell.

"One minute left," the referee yelled.

Here I am again, Darrell thought. The boy's grip tightened, and Darrell felt himself being thrown to his side. *This is what I wanted to stop, but here I am again. I'm still losing.* The thought filled him with a spark of anger. He had not been going to practice for a month so he could sit in front of his mother and lose.

The boy drove into Darrell, rolling him towards his back. One of Darrell's shoulderblades touched the mat. He knew he was about to be pinned.

"That's two points for Lincoln," the referee said.

"Darrell, get up!" Coach yelled.

Fans on the Lincoln side of the gym cheered.

"I gotta stop this!" bubbled a voice from inside Darrell. "I gotta do something."

Darrell noticed the boy was preparing to drive him sideways, to flip him up and pin him. Coach Lewis had taught the team a counter move in practice. To use it, Darrell would have to roll with the force of his opponent's drive. If he timed it right, the boy's own force would carry him right over, leaving Darrell above him and in control. It was Darrell's only chance.

The boy leaned back and drove with all his force into Darrell's side to flip him. Darrell rolled with the same drive. Without the resistance of Darrell's body, the Lincoln boy's force carried him right over Darrell. Immediately the boys switched positions. Darrell now was over his opponent. Quickly, he started wrapping the boy into a cradle of his own.

The Bluford crowd roared. The referee signalled that Darrell scored a point, but then he blew the whistle. The match was over. Darrell had lost by two points. As he walked back to his teammates, Coach Lewis came over to him.

"Good first match, Darrell. You would have had that Lincoln boy beat if you had another minute. But he beat you because you stopped trying in the second round. Remember that. You can't win if you don't do anything. Then you're just defeating yourself and your opponent doesn't have to work at all. As soon as you used your head and started wrestling him, you turned everything around. Keep that in mind, Darrell. Next time, I want you to use your head for the entire match—not just the last minute. Okay?"

Darrell nodded. The advice sounded familiar. It was what he read weeks ago in *Hatchet*. Brian had said the same thing about surviving and about change. It was the same idea that got Darrell to join the wrestling team in the first place. In order to win, to change, to succeed, you have to work at it. That was what the coach had said. That was what he had read in *Hatchet.* He thought of Amberlynn and Tyray. *I still have work to do,* he thought. *Lots of work.*

He was relieved that his first match was finally over. As odd as it sounded to him, he was a Bluford wrestler. For a moment, he felt proud. *At least I wasn't completely humiliated, and I even had a chance to win,* he thought. He was eager to practice harder. He wanted to be Bluford's best wrestler.

For the rest of the evening, Darrell watched the other members of his team wrestle. In the crowd he spotted Amberlynn and Jamee. They did not seem to notice him, but he remembered what Amberlynn said, how she loved to watch wrestling. Looking at her talking to Jamee, Darrell knew he had to go to the dance. Even if Tyray would be there, he had to go. Otherwise, he thought, it would be just like what Coach Lewis said. If he did not do anything, he would just be defeating himself.

After the match, Darrell met his mother and his Uncle Jason.

"Darrell, I am so proud of you. You looked great out there," his mother said, giving him a hug. The three of them left the building and started walking back home from Bluford.

"Yeah, Darrell. You looked pretty good for a few minutes," Uncle Jason added. "But that boy had you beat. You've got to improve your strength if you want to win on the mat."

Darrell looked over at his uncle. He knew part of what Uncle Jason said was right, but he resented him for saying it. *Why do you always want to make me feel bad?* Darrell wanted to ask. Instead he said, "It was my first match. The coach said it was good for my first time."

His uncle nodded. "He's right. But you can't just roll around and expect to win. When I wrestled, we had a guy on the team who flopped around in almost every match, never doing anything to win. We used to call him 'Fish' cause all he did was flipflop on the mat like a fish out of water." Uncle Jason laughed. "We teased him every day about that. I don't want you wrestlin' like ol' Fish."

"Darrell, I think you were great," his mother cut in. "I was proud to be your momma."

Darrell could barely hear her. His mind was still on what his uncle had said. Uncle Jason's comment made him feel as though all the work he had done for the past month was for nothing. He imagined what he must have looked like on the mat, how foolish he seemed in front of Amberlynn. Nothing had changed. He was still the same scared kid from Philadelphia. Rage boiled in his chest. He hated his uncle for robbing him of the one moment when he was almost pleased with himself. Darrell wished Uncle Jason had not come to the match. He wished he was not his uncle. As Darrell fought to control his temper, his uncle continued talking.

"And one more thing, Darrell. The way you—"

"You ain't my coach," Darrell interrupted. They had reached his uncle's driveway.

"What?" Uncle Jason asked. He turned his head to look at his nephew.

"You ain't my coach, so I don't need your advice, okay?"

"Darrell, don't you be rude to your uncle! He's only trying to help you," his mother snapped.

"I didn't ask for his help, Mom. Look at me! Do I need to hear from him that I look bad on the mat? Do I need to be told that I'm no good? I know it already.

He don't need to say it." Darrell stormed towards the apartment door.

Uncle Jason stood there in the driveway, shaking his head. "I'm only trying to give the boy some pointers. That's all. What's his problem, Jackie?"

Darrell slammed the door behind him. He was not going to talk to his uncle again.

Chapter 10

The next day at lunch, Darrell was eating with Harold.

"I heard about your match last night against Lincoln," Harold said.

"I lost," Darrell replied bitterly.

"I heard you were good, though."

"Who told you that?"

"I heard kids talking in homeroom."

Darrell grunted. His uncle's words haunted him.

"You know, I'm thinking about joining wrestling because of you, Darrell." Harold stared at him. "At first I didn't think you'd stick with it, but you did. Not only that, you look bigger and you seem . . . stronger. I'm thinking that wrestling could do the same for me," Harold confessed.

Darrell thought Harold was only saying things he thought Darrell needed to hear. But the look in his eyes told Darrell that his friend was serious. Darrell did not know what to say. Harold was the only kid Darrell knew who could understand what he was going through. For him to say what he did meant a lot.

"You should join," Darrell said to his friend. "Hey, if I can do it, you can do it."

As they ate, the boys watched one of the cafeteria workers on the other side of the room cleaning a mess of spilled vegetables on the floor. The woman looked like someone's grandmother. She seemed to have trouble bending to pick up the last of the mess. Whenever she leaned over, she rested one of her hands on her back as if it was sore. Darrell felt sorry that she had such a hard job. He remembered how Harold's grandmother had helped him pick up oranges the day Tyray attacked him on the street. He got up to help her.

Since he arrived at the high school, Darrell had rarely ventured to the other side of the cafeteria. Like other kids at Bluford, he and Harold sat at the same table each day. Besides, Darrell knew that Tyray and his friends sat at a table in the far corner of the cafeteria. As he approached the mess, he saw several people from the wrestling team. He had never noticed before that they were in his lunch period. Craig and Luis were at one table with some other students. Farther back, Kevin was sitting with an attractive girl.

Darrell bent down to help the old woman with the mess.

"Oh, thank you," she said. "I don't usually get help, and my back has been givin' me trouble the last few months. What's your name? I've never seen you before."

"I'm Darrell Mercer," he replied, cleaning up the last of the spilled vegetables.

"Well, Darrell, you can call me Miss Bea," she said with a smile. "Tell your momma she did a good job with you."

"Thanks."

Darrell wanted to sit with his friends from the team, but he knew that would leave Harold alone. When he returned to his table, Harold was smiling.

"What are you smiling at?" Darrell asked.

"When you got up to help Miss Bea, Amberlynn was watching you the whole time. I can tell by the way she was looking that she likes you. Darrell, you just gotta do something about that!"

There were those words again, Darrell thought. *Do something.* The same words that Coach Lewis had screamed to him in the wrestling match. Almost automatically, Darrell heard himself responding to Harold.

"I am gonna talk to Amberlynn at the dance this Friday," he said.

"For real?" Harold exclaimed, looking shocked.

"Yeah, I'm gonna go." Darrell could barely believe his own words. He knew Harold was surprised. Less than two months ago, Darrell was a scared and lonely kid who wanted to run back to Philadelphia. Now he was on the wrestling team and preparing to go to a dance to meet a girl.

But each Friday when he paid Tyray, he felt as scared as he did during his first days at Bluford. That had not changed. Deep inside, Darrell knew that what he wanted would not come until he confronted Tyray, that nothing would be different as long as he kept paying him. But he was afraid to stop. Tyray and his friends would come after him if the money stopped, and Darrell knew he would have nowhere to hide. Thinking about it made Darrell shudder.

"Well, then, I'll go too," Harold said, breaking Darrell's thoughts. "I've never been to a dance before." Then he added shyly, "Maybe Cindy Gibson will be there too."

"Cindy Gibson? Who's that?"

"She lives down the hall from my apartment. She's friends with Jamee and Amberlynn."

"Well, if Jamee and Amberlynn are going, she'll probably be there too."

"I hope so," Harold smiled.

The two boys shook hands and agreed they would go to the dance together.

At 8:00 Friday evening, Darrell and Harold met in front of Bluford. Dozens of students were streaming into the school when they arrived. Some were dropped off from cars and others were walking in large groups. Darrell and Harold joined a crowd heading down the school's main hallway towards the cafeteria.

Several police officers as well as a handful of parents and teachers lined the hallways to make sure there would be no trouble at the dance. One of the teachers was Mr. Mitchell. Seeing so many adults made Darrell feel safer.

"Look at that!" Harold said, pointing

forward. A police officer with a metal detector was up ahead of them. People were being checked for guns and knives before being let into the dance.

"Man, it looks like a prison, not a school," Darrell replied. Still, he was grateful people were being checked for weapons. *At least Tyray won't have his knife,* he thought.

As they neared the cafeteria, Darrell felt the deep rhythmic thumping of dance music growing stronger and stronger. Just outside the cafeteria doors, he could feel the beat vibrating in his chest and stomach. Darrell was nervous. He wondered if Amberlynn would even be there.

"I hope Cindy is here," Harold said suddenly.

"Yeah, I know what you're sayin'. I hope Amberlynn's here, or I'm gonna feel pretty stupid," Darrell replied. "She's the reason I'm here."

The cafeteria was rapidly filling up with kids. All the lunch tables had been cleared out to make a giant dance floor, and snowflakes and other winter decorations had been taped to the walls. Every minute, more and more kids arrived. Darrell recognized some from his classes.

Soon the cafeteria was nearly as full

as it was at lunchtime. Some students were starting to dance. Darrell looked for Amberlynn, but he could not find her. He decided to buy a soda.

Darrell pulled a crumpled ten-dollar bill from his pocket. Before he left, his mother had told him he looked handsome. Then, adding that he should have fun, she gave him the money. As he paid for the drink, Darrell realized it was the first time in months that he had money which was not going to Tyray. He imagined the smirk on Tyray's face each time Darrell gave him his mother's money. He wished he would never see that smirk again. He shoved the change into his pocket and went back to join Harold.

The dance floor continued to fill up. So many people had arrived that it was impossible to see over the crowd to the other side of the cafeteria. Darrell guessed that there were several hundred people in the crowd, maybe more. He worried that Amberlynn might not come after all.

"Look, there she is," Harold said, pointing. "Over there."

Jamee and Amberlynn were weaving through the crowd to get to the dance floor. Darrell's heart raced.

"Man, she looks *good!*" Harold exclaimed. He took a gulp of Darrell's soda. "So whatcha gonna do?"

Darrell shrugged. He was nervous. Wearing a snug blue dress for the dance, Amberlynn looked like a model out of a magazine. She also looked like someone who would never be interested in a guy like him, he thought. "I don't know, Harold. Look at her."

"You mean you came all this way so you could talk to her, and now you're not gonna do anything except sit here? Get over there. I saw the way she looked at you at lunch. Go over and talk to her," Harold demanded.

Just then Darrell saw Cindy walk by with a few of her friends. "Hey, there's Cindy," he said.

Harold turned to look at her. Darrell could tell by the expression on Harold's face that he was suddenly nervous too. "So what are *you* gonna do?" he asked.

Harold smiled and shrugged his shoulders.

Darrell knew Harold was right. He had to try to talk to Amberlynn, but he had no idea what he would say. He imagined himself stuttering and making a fool of himself. How could he ever go near her?

But a voice in his head told him he had to. If he did not talk to her, the voice said, he would be defeating himself again. If he wanted something to happen, *he had to do something.* When he imagined her laughing at him, he cringed. But when he imagined himself being too scared to approach her, he hated himself. He was tired of being scared. In either case, he realized he would not end up with Amberlynn. But if he spoke to her, at least he would know that he was not letting his fear beat him. He started walking over towards her.

"Where you going, Darrell?" Harold asked.

Darrell kept walking. He did not want anything to stop him.

He saw her in front of a group of students. She was saying something to Jamee as he approached them. Jamee saw him first.

"Hey, Darrell. What's up?" Jamee asked with a wide grin on her face. "Uh, Amberlynn, I'm gonna go get something to drink. I'll be right back," she said. Then she left.

Darrell looked at Amberlynn. She smiled at him.

"Hi, Darrell," she said warmly. "I saw you wrestle the other day. You looked so good out there. I couldn't believe it was your first match."

"Thanks," Darrell said. He did not know what to say to her. Maybe what Jamee said was true, he thought. Maybe she did like him. "I still have a lot to learn," he said. He was embarrassed about losing, but she did not seem to hold it against him.

"Look, Darrell, I've been meaning to talk to you. I'm sorry about what happened that day in English class with Tyray. I felt horrible. I should have never said what I did about you," she said. Darrell was surprised at how sincere she sounded.

"Amberlynn, I'm the one who should be sorry," Darrell replied. "I brought all that on you. I wish it never happened." He shook his head.

"Why don't we just put it behind us, okay?" Amberlynn said.

"Deal," Darrell said. He noticed the music had softened and people were pairing up to dance in couples. "You wanna dance?" he asked. He could not believe that he had said it. He was almost certain she would laugh.

"Yeah," she answered. "I was hoping you'd ask."

Darrell put his arms around Amberlynn's waist and pulled her gently to him. He noticed that he was about as tall as she was, though when they first met, she seemed a bit taller. As he danced, he felt her warm hands around his neck. He did not want the dance to end. But then he saw a familiar face through the corner of his eye.

Rodney was standing at the edge of the crowd of dancers. He was watching them, a tight-lipped grin plastered on his face.

Darrell knew that if Rodney was around, Tyray was not far away. His pulse started to pound. He was not sure what to do. He did not want to tell Amberlynn he was afraid, but he did not want to cause another embarrassing moment for her like the one in English class. The slow song was ending and a faster song was already starting. Darrell knew he had to get away from Amberlynn or else both of them would be targets.

"Amberlynn . . . I'll . . . be right back," Darrell said.

"Where are you going?" she asked. He could tell by the look on her face that she was confused.

"I have to tell Harold something. I'll be right back." He walked back to where he had been standing when he arrived at the dance. He could not see Harold or Rodney. The cafeteria was dark except for a few weak lights over the dance floor. Crowds of students seemed to bounce and sway in unison, and the beat of the music grew louder and more intense. Darrell felt like he was trapped inside a giant heart that pumped and throbbed around him. He was scared. The only idea he could think of was to find Mr. Mitchell. But he did not know what he could say even if he found him. Nothing had happened. Not yet.

Darrell was moving quickly towards the hallway when he felt a large hand grip the back of his neck.

"Why you in such a hurry, midget man? You and me got some talkin' to do." It was Tyray.

Tyray steered him forward. Darrell was not sure where he was going until he was shoved into the men's room. Several other kids came in. One of them stood outside the door to stop other kids from going in.

"How much money did your momma give you tonight?" Tyray asked.

"I ain't got no money," Darrell said.

"Boy, don't you lie to me! I ain't

playin' games with you. I know you're sweatin' Amberlynn. I can make you the biggest fool in this high school. And I'll drag her down there with you. She won't ever look at your sorry face again, and the rest of the school will laugh every time you walk in a room." Tyray stepped closer. "Man, everybody already knows you're a scared little punk. What they don't know is that you been payin' me each week. When I tell everyone that, people will laugh so loud, they'll hear about you and your poor sorry momma all the way back in Philly. Now whatcha gonna do?" Tyray growled.

Darrell hated Tyray, but he feared him more. Three of Tyray's friends, including Rodney, were in the bathroom. Darrell was cornered. He hoped a teacher would walk in and rescue him, but he was alone. He could not bear to think of what Amberlynn would say if she knew he gave money to Tyray each week. But most importantly, Darrell did not want Tyray to make fun of her.

Slowly he reached into his pocket and pulled out his mother's change.

"See, he ain't as stupid as he looks," Tyray said, creeping even closer to Darrell and grabbing the money.

"Your momma must be real proud of you," Rodney added with a chuckle.

"Now about Amberlynn," Tyray said, gripping Darrell's arm. Tyray's friends also grabbed him, their arms like thick ropes preventing him from escaping. Darrell struggled, but he was unable to free himself from the three boys' grasp. They yanked him over to the back of the bathroom where a large trash can stood.

"Let go of me!" Darrell yelled.

The boys lifted him off the ground and dropped him head first into the trash can. Darrell's face landed on a pile of wet paper towels and empty soda cans. Darrell winced at the heavy scent of orange soda and the chemical detergent the janitors used to clean the bathroom.

"You ain't nothin' but trash, Darrell. Remember that. Stay away from Amberlynn, or next time, it'll be worse," Tyray said. Darrell heard footsteps and then the sound of the bathroom door closing.

Enraged, Darrell tried to pull himself from the can. With one great push, he managed to tip the trash can over, and he and all its contents spilled out onto the bathroom floor. Darrell stood up amidst the trash and saw his reflection in the mirror. Bits of paper were caught in his hair, and a soda stain marked his white shirt. Tears welled in his eyes. He never felt worse. Tyray and his friends were taking everything from him. And he was still too weak to protect himself. Wrestling had not helped him at all.

A group of boys came in to use the bathroom.

"Man, look at this guy," one of them said. Another one laughed.

Darrell stared into the mirror. A tear rolled off his face and dripped onto the tile floor. Darrell wanted to scream. He wanted to yell as loud as he could at the world for what it allowed to happen to him, for how it allowed Tyray to get away with everything. He wanted to curse God for allowing his world to be filled with so much torment. Darrell kicked the trash can, sending it smashing against the bathroom wall.

Then, as the other boys left, Harold walked in.

"Darrell, where you been? Amber-lynn is looking . . . . What happened to you? Why you got trash in your hair?"

"Leave me alone!" Darrell screamed, rushing out of the bathroom. He shoul-dered his way through the crowd, stormed down the hallway and made his way out of the school. He started to sprint as fast as his feet could carry him. He wanted to get away forever from the people who laughed when they saw him, who humiliated him when they got the chance. Darrell sprinted the mile back to his home, tears streaking down his face. The lights were out when he got back to the apartment. He went into his dark room, sat on his bed and quietly wept.

Chapter 11

On Monday, Darrell did not have to go back to school except for wrestling practice. The winter recess had come, and Bluford High was closed for the Christmas and New Year's holidays. Darrell was grateful he did not have to set foot in a classroom for a while. He did not want to see Amberlynn. He was sure she was mad at him for leaving her at the dance. He wondered if she found out why he had left so suddenly. If she did, she was probably ashamed of what a coward he was. Still, Darrell was glad about one thing. At least he had spared Amberlynn from Tyray's teasing.

Darrell and his mother spent Christmas Day with Uncle Jason's family. Despite a delicious dinner of fried chicken and mashed garlic potatoes and receiving a new outfit from his uncle and aunt,

Darrell couldn't wait to get home, away from his cousins' constant bickering.

It was the first Christmas Darrell had spent away from Philadelphia and his friends. Later that evening, in the quiet of his own living room, Darrell remembered how he and Malik used to compare presents right after the holiday. He wondered if Malik would like the new Nike warm-up jacket his mother got him for Christmas. It seemed like years had passed since he stood on his street with his old friends. He was thinking about the last time he had seen Malik when his mother sat down next to him.

"Darrell, is everything okay in school?" she asked. "I know I've been busy lately, but I am a little concerned about you." She watched him as she spoke.

He wondered why she seemed so worried. Maybe she had figured out what he was doing with the lunch money. Or maybe she wanted to know what he had done with the change he had from the dance. He did not want to lie to her, but he did not want to tell her the truth either.

"You seem to be doing so well. Your grades are better this marking period." It was true, Darrell thought. He had done better in school since he joined the wrestling team. "Jason and I are so proud that you are wrestling, and I was happy to see that you wanted to go to the dance. That takes a lot of courage, especially for someone new to the school. But with all that, you still don't seem happy. You walk around like you got something on your mind all the time. And every time I ask you, you say, 'I'm fine, Mom,'" she said.

Darrell turned away from his mother. He wanted to tell her the truth about the money and about Tyray, but he could not bring himself to do it. He just did not want her to worry, and he did not want her to tell Uncle Jason. He would only make Darrell feel worse about everything.

"It's just hard, Mom," he said, fighting to stay calm. "It's hard to get used to things out here . . . but I'm okay."

"Baby, if I can do anything for you, let me know. You're not alone," she said. Then she gave him a hug.

But I am, Mom, he thought. *I am alone. Who else is here with me?*

Two days after Christmas, Darrell came home from wrestling practice and heard a noise coming from his uncle's garage. It sounded like kids yelling. He put his head up to the door and listened.

"Lemme out!" a child cried. Darrell could tell it was his cousin Nate's voice.

"You gonna give me the remote control car you got for Christmas?" a second voice said. It was Travis.

"Lemme out! I can't breathe!" Nate screamed. There was terror in his voice.

"Give me the car, and I'll let you out," Travis yelled back.

"Please let me out! Somebody help me!"

Darrell yanked open the garage door.

In the dim light, he saw Travis sitting on an old wooden trunk that was padlocked shut. The sound of Nate's sobbing was coming from inside the trunk. Though it was dark, Darrell could see Travis's eyes glistening slightly. "Let me out!" Nate begged.

Darrell felt Nate's pain. But what froze Darrell for a second was Travis. In his cousin's young face, Darrell saw Tyray. He spotted his hateful smirk lurking maybe just a few years away. Darrell knew that if no one confronted and stopped him, Travis would grow up to be another Tyray. Darrell could not sit still.

He could not allow a bully to get away with hurting another kid, especially in his own family. Despite what Uncle Jason had said, Darrell could not let Travis torture his brother.

"Leave him alone!" Darrell yelled and walked into the garage. "Let him out of there now."

"My dad said not to listen to you. You can't tell me what to do," Travis said defiantly.

Darrell did not care what his uncle said. In one swift move, he yanked Travis off the trunk and pushed him firmly into the wall of the garage. "Give me the key to the trunk," Darrell growled.

Travis looked surprised. "Let me go!" he screamed. "I'm gonna tell my dad."

Darrell saw a shiny metal key in Travis's hand and grabbed it. Quickly he unlocked the trunk and helped Nate out.

"My dad's gonna kick you outta your house and fire your momma. You'll be poor like you were before you got here!"

Just then Uncle Jason's deep voice bellowed through the garage. "What's the problem in here?"

"Dad, Darrell's pushing me around," Travis whined.

"He locked Nate in the trunk and wouldn't let him out until he gave away his Christmas present," Darrell explained.

Uncle Jason looked shocked. "You do that, Travis?" he asked.

Travis trembled.

"He did, Dad," Nate insisted. "He stuck me in the trunk, and I couldn't breathe, and he wouldn't let me out 'cause he wanted my car. I was scared—"

"He's lying!" Travis howled.

A terrible look came over his uncle's face, as if he saw something horrible that he had never wanted to admit existed. He walked over to his older son. "What do you think you are doin', boy? You could have choked your brother in there."

Travis shrugged his shoulders and looked at the ground.

"Don't you *ever* try to hurt your brother again, you hear me! Just 'cause you are bigger don't give you the right to push him around or take things from him. I ain't raisin' no bullies in this house," Uncle Jason yelled. "Now we are gonna get this mess straightened out. Both of you get in the house. I'll be there when I'm done with Darrell. And I'll say this once, Travis, you better tell me the truth 'cause if I find out you are lying, you might not come outside again until next Christmas! Now get inside." Both brothers ran into the house. Uncle Jason looked over at Darrell.

"I'm glad you were here, Darrell," he said. "I know I told you not to get involved with them, but you did the right thing. A man's got to stand up when someone else is in trouble, even if it means he might get himself into trouble."

Darrell could tell his uncle was struggling to find the right words. He liked that Uncle Jason had called him a man.

"Look," his uncle continued, "I'm sorry I upset you at your first wrestling match, Darrell." He paused awkwardly. "Maybe you don't need my help, but maybe I need yours. You showed me that I need to pay more attention to what's happening with my boys." He stopped again and looked at the trunk that Nate had been trapped in. "You're a good kid, Darrell. You are coming along just fine," he said quietly and walked into the house.

Darrell was stunned. He stood in the garage after his uncle left. He quietly closed the trunk, laid the key on top, and went home. For years, Uncle Jason had made him feel smaller and weaker. When he was a young boy, Darrell had dreaded his uncle's visits to Philadelphia. But now things were suddenly different. For once, his uncle said something good about him. For once, he seemed to respect him. At first, Darrell could not understand why Uncle Jason had acted so differently, but the more he thought about it, the more it started to make sense. Darrell *was* different from the person he had been a few months ago.

Two months ago, he raced home every day to hide from Tyray. Now he stayed after school to go to wrestling practice. Six weeks ago, he could not even climb halfway up the ropes in practice. Now he could reach the top every time. During his first weeks at Bluford his grades were low C's. Now they were all B's. When he arrived in California, he knew no one. Now he was friends with Harold, danced once with Amberlynn, and talked regularly with the guys on the wrestling team, even older guys like Kevin. What made him even happier was that he had grown an inch since he got to Bluford. He *was* different, he realized, but not different enough. Darrell still lived in fear of Tyray. He still paid him every Friday. And, worst of all, he allowed his fear of Tyray to keep him away from Amberlynn Bailey, the only girl he liked at Bluford.

The day before New Year's, Darrell won a wrestling match for the first time by beating a freshman from Sterling High School, 8 to 2. Coach Lewis was so happy that he hugged Darrell when he stepped off the mat.

"You'll be varsity by your junior year if you keep working this hard," he said. Kevin told him that he seemed to be learning faster than even he had.

That night, his mother bought him his favorite ice cream, mint chocolate chip, and the two sat on the couch and ate it together.

At midnight, she told him she wanted to give up fast food in the new year. "I'm gonna get big if I don't watch myself," she said. "How about you? Any changes you want to make for the new year?"

Darrell just smiled and shook his head. He wanted to keep his New Year's resolution to himself. But he knew what it was. It had been building since the moment he handed his mother's money to Tyray. It had continued to grow since he read *Hatchet*, since he joined the wrestling team, since he held Amberlynn close to him at the Freshman Dance. He just had not been ready before. But he was now.

He was going to stop paying Tyray.

Chapter 12

The first Friday of the new year,
Darrell did not walk to the supermarket
parking lot to meet Tyray. Instead he
took the back street to school.

Darrell pictured Tyray and Rodney
standing by the supermarket waiting for
him. He wondered what they would
think when they realized he was not
going to meet them. Darrell could almost
hear Tyray yelling and cursing.

Darrell knew Tyray and Rodney
would try to get the money from him
somehow. But he was not going to pay
them again—even if Tyray hurt him.
Darrell had decided that his days in
school were miserable whether he paid
Tyray or not. So why pay him? He had
been humiliated since he arrived at
Bluford. He had lost a chance with
Amberlynn, and he had been robbed of

his mother's money for weeks. What more could they do?

When Darrell arrived in school, he felt better than he had in months. Knowing the lunch money was in *his* pocket—not Tyray's—made his whole day more cheerful. He had decided on New Year's Day that he would use the money to buy his own lunch in the cafeteria. For the first time in weeks, Darrell did not carry sandwiches in his backpack. Even though he did not like most of the food at Bluford, he knew today's lunch would be one of the best he ever had.

Darrell got to English class early. Tyray and Rodney had not arrived yet, and Darrell wondered if they were still looking for him at the supermarket. As he waited for Mr. Mitchell to come into the classroom, Darrell could tell that Amberlynn was watching him. He had been avoiding her all week, even though she looked like she wanted to talk to him whenever they made eye contact. He was still embarrassed about the dance, but he chose to avoid her because he knew Tyray would tease her if he saw them talking.

Tyray and Rodney arrived in class at the same time. As they walked up the aisle to their desks, Tyray stopped next to Darrell.

"Where were you this morning? You owe me ten dollars. Now you're gonna have to pay extra, or I'll bust your head after school today," he whispered. A droplet of Tyray's spit landed on Darrell's face. Just then Mr. Mitchell came in, and Tyray moved to his desk. For the rest of the class, Darrell tried to ignore what Tyray had said. He did not know what he would do when Tyray confronted him. He was tired of running. But he was still scared.

At lunchtime, Darrell joined Harold in the food line.

"You didn't pack lunch today?" Harold asked. Darrell had never told his friend the full truth about why he always packed his lunch.

"Nope," Darrell replied. Though the two had been back at school for a few days, Harold had not asked Darrell what happened at the dance. Darrell figured Harold was waiting to see if he would mention it. He still did not want to.

"You picked a bad day to buy lunch. Look at that stuff," Harold joked.

A server passed Darrell a plate full of meatloaf that looked like a brown sponge covered in chunky brown gravy. Next to the meatloaf was a mushy glob of mashed potatoes and some over-cooked peas and carrots. Both boys grabbed a large cup of soda, paid for their food and began making their way back towards their table.

Suddenly, Darrell saw Tyray walking towards him. Darrell's heart raced. He had nowhere to go.

At first, Tyray looked as if he might pass right by Darrell, but as he got near-er he pretended to trip. In one swift motion, Tyray fell forward, reached an arm under Darrell's tray, and flipped it.

The tray spilled onto Darrell's body, dumping mashed potatoes, gravy, and vegetables all over his clothes and then falling into a large slippery mess at his feet. Soda and ice splashed all over his pants.

The tray hit the cafeteria floor with a loud crash. For a second, the usual mur-mur of the cafeteria hushed as students looked to see what happened. Everyone in the lunchroom turned towards the sound. They all stared at Darrell. Then, in a snap, the noise returned. Some stu-dents clapped in mock applause. Others, especially those at Tyray's table, began laughing loudly. Darrell sensed people were watching him, eager to see what he would do next. The room grew charged, like the air before a bad storm.

"Whoops, sorry about that," Tyray said with a grin and walked off towards his friends.

Darrell picked up the tray and walked over to his seat across from Harold. He grabbed some napkins and started wiping the food from his shirt. He saw Amberlynn watching him from her table. She looked concerned. Darrell hated that she had seen what happened. He wanted to talk to her and explain why he left her at the dance, that he was trying to protect her from Tyray. But he could not talk to her now, not with food dripping down his shirt.

Darrell was about to get a new tray of food when he saw Miss Bea, the nice old woman who worked in the lunchroom, coming out to clean up the spilled food. Darrell watched as she struggled to move a heavy yellow bucket filled with soapy water. He could see by the look on her face that she was in pain. He remembered how she said her back had been sore for months. Darrell watched as she slowly stooped over to pick up the larger pieces of food by hand. He could almost hear her old bones groaning. Anger started to bubble inside Darrell.

Darrell got up to help her. He was sick of what always happened at Bluford, at how everyone seemed to ignore how Tyray hurt others like Miss Bea, Amberlynn, or himself. Darrell thought of the time at the dance, the days in the locker room, and now in the lunchroom. *Too many times, people look the other way when they should be doing something*, Darrell thought. He remembered his uncle's words. *A man's got to stand up when someone else is in trouble, even if it means he might get himself into trouble.*

Darrell leaned over and scooped up a piece of the spilled meatloaf. As he threw away the greasy chunk, he glanced over at Tyray and his friends at their lunch table. They were laughing wildly and pointing at him. Rodney was almost rolling out of his chair with laughter.

"Look at that fool!" Tyray shouted. "Maybe that's his poor momma. No wonder he ain't got no money." His friends erupted in laughter.

Miss Bea did not seem to notice what was being said. "Thanks for helping," she said softly to Darrell.

Darrell felt as if his chest was about to explode. He never felt so furious, so frustrated. Brian's words from *Hatchet* echoed deep inside him. *Do something,* they said. *If you want a change, you've got to do something to get it.*

"You better save that food, fool. 'Cause you ain't buyin' lunch again," Tyray called out.

Darrell looked down into the mess of spilled soda and mashed potatoes. He saw his own reflection in the brown puddle. Nearby, Miss Bea strained to lift the water-filled mop out of the bucket. Something inside Darrell snapped. He stared at Tyray.

"Just shut up, Tyray!" Darrell yelled.

Tyray turned his head towards Darrell. He looked stunned. His friends stopped laughing.

Kids at surrounding tables who had already forgotten about the spilled tray now looked again at Darrell.

"What you say, fool?" Tyray asked.

"I said shut your mouth."

"Boy, are you high or somethin'? You better sit down, or I'm gonna come over there and hurt you," Tyray said, standing up. Two of his friends stood up with him.

"Tyray, you ain't nothing but a bully," Darrell said, pausing for a moment. The rest of the cafeteria seemed to groan at Darrell's words. "No one in this school likes you. They are just afraid of you. But you know what? I ain't afraid of you no more. You don't scare me." Darrell's pulse throbbed. He felt more alive than ever. He knew Tyray could beat him, but it did not matter. He was being more honest than he had ever been in his entire life. It felt exciting and powerful.

Nearby, students started chanting. "Fight! Fight! Fight!"

Miss Bea backed away. She had seen cafeteria fights before. Darrell knew the lunch monitors would arrive soon to break things up, but right now, he did not care what happened.

Tyray moved quickly over to Darrell. Rodney and two other friends were right behind him. The boys stood around the mess left by the spilled tray.

"You got a big mouth for such a little man. It's a shame I'm gonna have to break it for you." Tyray shoved Darrell. Tyray's friends started to move on either side of Darrell, but suddenly they stopped. Darrell looked back to see Kevin, Luis, and Craig standing behind him.

"We got your back, Darrell," Kevin said. Tyray's friends did not challenge

Kevin. From now on, the fight was between Darrell and Tyray. No one else was welcome.

"You gotta stop, Tyray. You been pushing people around for too long. It ain't happenin' no more. Now why don't you apologize to Miss Bea and help clean up the mess you made," Darrell said. A large group of students formed a circle around the two boys. Everyone was scrambling to get the best position to see what would happen next. Darrell felt like he was in the beginning of another wrestling match.

"Fight! Fight! Fight!" The chants continued.

"So whatcha gonna do about it, little man?" Tyray scoffed, his eyes locked on Darrell's face. Then his lip curled into a smirk.

Darrell gazed at him. Even if the lunch monitors were on their way, it would take them a few minutes to clear away all the students.

For a moment, the two boys stared at each other in silence. Then Tyray glanced to his side. The glance was slight, as fast as the blink of an eye. To the crowd of students surrounding them, the tiny twitch might have been invisible, but not to Darrell. He saw it and knew what it meant. His body trembled with excitement. He had not been stared down.

Tyray's friends had backed away, and now he was alone facing Darrell with dozens of students watching. As the seconds passed, Darrell sensed something new in his eyes, something he recognized well. Beneath the cold smirk on Tyray's face, Darrell saw fear. His heart raced.

Then Tyray shoved him. "Boy, get outta my face! I've had enough of you."

The force of the shove threw Darrell back. He nearly lost his footing in the slippery mess. Tyray was definitely stronger than he was, but Darrell was stronger than he used to be. Two months ago, he would have fallen. Now, he was just pushed back. Darrell knew he could not beat Tyray physically. But somehow Darrell felt as if he had already beaten him.

"Fight! Fight! Fight!"

"Clean up the mess and apologize to Miss Bea. That's all you gotta do," Darrell demanded.

"Break it up! Break it up!" yelled a teacher's voice from somewhere in the distance. Students reluctantly started moving away from the circle.

"You're goin' down, boy!" Tyray screamed. He lunged at Darrell like a cornered animal.

Instinctively, Darrell dodged Tyray's charge, using the speed he had gained through wrestling to move out of the larger boy's way.

"I'm gonna kill you!" Tyray growled and threw several punches at Darrell's face. Darrell avoided two of them, but the third one glanced off the side of his cheekbone. Over Tyray's shoulder, Darrell could see teachers struggling to make their way into the center of the fight.

"You want some more, little man? You gonna get it," Tyray said.

Tyray came at him again. This time, Darrell decided not to fight Tyray, but to wrestle him. As Tyray came in, Darrell charged at him as if he were an opponent in a wrestling match. He decided to use his favorite wrestling move, the double leg takedown. In one quick motion, Darrell darted underneath Tyray and locked his arms around Tyray's legs.

"What are you doin', fool?" Tyray yelled. The two were so close that Tyray had no room to punch him. Instead, he tried pounding on Darrell's back.

Darrell felt Tyray's fists slamming into his back, but the blows did not have much force. Ignoring them, Darrell quickly hoisted Tyray into the air.

"Let me go," Tyray yelled, his feet off the ground.

"Okay," said Darrell. Finishing the takedown, he tossed Tyray to his side and sent the bully crashing down into the cafeteria floor. Just as he let Tyray go, Darrell saw him put his hand down to cushion his fall. Then he heard a loud, wet snap and a scream.

Tyray was on the ground, squirming and rolling in the spilled food. He was holding his wrist. "It's broke. It's broke," he cried. Soda and mashed potatoes covered his face, and meatloaf was smeared all over his pants. A few bits of vegetables were caught in his hair. "It's broke," he whimpered. "You broke it!"

"Break it up," a teacher yelled, seizing Darrell. Three other teachers moved the crowd of students back. Mr. Mitchell was one of them. Quickly, he glanced at Darrell and then went to help Tyray. Rodney and the rest of Tyray's friends were silent. They looked stunned. All of them were sent to the principal's office. Darrell knew he would probably be suspended, but he did not care. For the first time at Bluford, Darrell felt free.

He had toppled the bully.

In the principal's office, with Mr. Mitchell and Coach Lewis behind him, Darrell told the truth about what had happened since he arrived at Bluford. He explained that he had been teased and tormented for weeks and admitted that he had been giving his lunch money to Tyray. He told everyone about the crushed oranges, the events in the locker room, and the time he was tossed into a trash can. He then described how Tyray knocked his lunch to the floor and how he could not allow Miss Bea to clean it up by herself. As he spoke, the tears came. They rolled freely down his face as he recounted all that had happened during his short time at the high school. They were tears of shame, anger, relief, and joy all mixed together, and he let them fall.

After a long closed-door meeting with Mr. Mitchell, Coach Lewis, and, for a short time, Miss Bea, the principal chose not to suspend Darrell. She informed him that she was suspending Tyray for three days and that she planned to have a meeting with both boys and their parents. Before she dismissed him, she made Darrell promise to tell her if anyone picked on him again. She also warned Darrell that if he got into another fight, she would be forced to suspend him. "Yes, ma'am," he replied.

Darrell appreciated that she was not suspending him, but he wondered if she knew how silly the threat of a suspension sounded. After what he had been through, no punishment the principal could give would be worse than the treatment he had already received from students. Holding onto this thought, he thanked the principal. She smiled warmly and dismissed him.

It was the end of the school day when Darrell finally left the principal's office. The main hallway was filling with students rushing to get to their lockers and go home. Darrell shouldered his way into the crowded corridor and headed towards his own locker on the other side of the school. Looking at the students around him, Darrell felt as if he were walking through a strange dream. Everything seemed familiar to him but somehow different.

Although he was physically tired, he was also strangely alert and calm at the same time. He also felt bigger, not just in relation to everyone else, but as if there were more of him, as if he had somehow added something to himself. It was as if the whole world had shrunk a bit during the time he had been in the principal's office.

Instead of rushing through the hallway as he normally did—with his head down—Darrell decided to slow down, to look at the people around him.

Something has definitely changed, Darrell thought as he made his way through the corridor. He could feel it in his bones, in every cell of his body. He was not the person who stepped off the bus from Philadelphia a few months ago. Bluford's once threatening hallways no longer frightened him. And Tyray, the bully who had tortured him for months, had diminished too.

Darrell knew he would face Tyray again. The meeting the principal had scheduled for the two boys and their parents would take place early next week. Besides that meeting, there were still months of shared English and gym classes ahead of them. There was also lunch. But now Darrell was not bothered by the thought of seeing Tyray. More powerful than the painful memories was a new memory—the look on Tyray's face when he cowered before Darrell on the cafeteria floor, clutching his shattered wrist. In that instant, Tyray's power over Darrell had been broken.

Darrell walked past the hallway where Tyray and Rodney once shoved him. He wondered what Tyray and his friends would do in the weeks to come. Would they seek revenge? Would someone else try to fill Tyray's shoes? Probably. It seemed no matter where he looked—in Philadelphia, at Bluford, on the news, or in his own family—there were always bullies and victims. But even if they came after him, it did not matter. Darrell would not remain quiet or give them money if they threatened him. He would not run away from them anymore.

Things are gonna be different around here, Darrell thought, leaving the old hallway behind him. And he was certain Tyray knew it, even as he sat in a nearby hospital having a cast made for his broken hand.

The crowds in the hallways were thinning as Darrell rounded the corner and went to his locker. Bending to grab his books, he heard some students gathering quietly beside him. He turned to face Amberlynn, Harold, and Kevin. The anxious looks on their faces showed that they cared about him.

"Hey guys," Darrell said. A smile spread across his face.

Amberlynn threw her arms around his shoulders and gave Darrell a warm hug. He closed his eyes and wrapped his arms around her.

Kevin slapped his back affectionately. "Nice takedown, Darrell," he said with a grin.

"Darrell Mercer, you're the *man!*" Harold yelled excitedly. "Everybody's saying that!"

Darrell was grateful for them. They were his friends, his *new* friends. Because of them, he would never again be alone at Bluford.

"Thanks for waiting for me," he said. He thought they deserved to know all that had happened over the past few months, and he wanted to tell them. But he knew if the words came, the tears would fall again. He could barely hold them back even as he thanked them. He decided he would tell them everything another day. "I mean it, guys. Thank you."

"You're the *man*!" Harold yelled again even louder than before. And Kevin slapped Darrell's back again.

"C'mon, let's get outta here," Amberlynn said, tugging Darrell by his shirt.

Looking at the three of them, Darrell knew the long nightmare that began when he left Philadelphia had finally ended, and a new day filled with hope and possibility had begun.

Together with his friends, he walked down the hall and out the front doors of Bluford High.

Discussion Guide to

BLUFORD HIGH

The Bully

by Paul Langan

Top Five Reasons Students Will Be Turned On to the Bluford High Series

1. This widely acclaimed teen series set in an urban high school features engaging, accessible writing and appealing, contemporary storylines.

2. These books are gripping, suspenseful, and intricate tales of high school. They deal with real, tangible issues that will feel familiar and immediate to teen readers.

3. They feature relatable characters with diverse backgrounds.

4. Important life lessons are woven into the stories' resolutions, but they are never preachy.

5. No matter how dramatic or tragic these stories feel, they all have a positive, hopeful ending.

Discussion Questions

Chapters 1 and 2

1. Why do you think Darrell doesn't like his mom to call him "baby"?

2. Do you agree with Mom's advice that Darrell should smile to make friends? Explain. How might Darrell make new friends?

3. What comments does Uncle Jason make when he sees Darrell? How does Darrell feel about how Uncle Jason regards him?

4. Darrell thinks he'll never be able to replace Malik and his other good friends in Philadelphia. What qualities do you look for in a close friend? Make a list of these qualities, and then compare your list with those of your classmates.

Chapters 3 and 4

1. What is Darrell's initial opinion of Mr. Mitchell? How does his opinion change? Why?

2. Do you agree that Uncle Jason is right to raise his boys by letting them

play rough? Why or why not? Before coming to a conclusion, make a list of the pros and cons of raising a child this way.

3. As he begins school at Bluford High, Darrell worries he'll never be "in" with the other kids. What do you think it takes to be "in"? Is being "in" important to you? Explain.

4. On the first day of school, Darrell especially worries about who he will sit with at lunch. Write a paper describing lunchtime in your school. Do certain kids sit with each other and avoid other people? Do you always sit with the same people? At the same table, or in the same area? If someone you did not know or someone new in your school asked to sit with you, how would you respond? How would you want someone to respond if you were in that situation?

Chapters 5 and 6

1. Contrast Mr. Mitchell and Mr. Dooling regarding how observant they

are about student behavior. Which of the two is more aware of what's really happening in his class? Give examples.

2. What does Darrell tell his mother when she asks him how school is going? Why does he reply as he does?

3. In Chapter 6, we are told, "Darrell and his friends made it a rule never to bring adults into their problems, especially teachers." Do you think this "rule" should apply to Darrell's current situation? In general, do you agree that young people should avoid talking to adults? Give examples of situations that do require adult involvement and ones that don't.

4. Darrell dreads going to gym class for a variety of reasons. Write about a particular class or subject at school that you really dislike. Be sure to discuss the various reasons why you don't enjoy that subject. At the end of your paper, discuss what could be done to improve your opinion of the class.

Chapters 7 and 8

1. What does Mr. Mitchell give Darrell to help him solve his problem? What is Darrell's opinion of Mr. Mitchell's advice?

2. How do the following people — Mom, Harold, Amberlynn, and Tyray — respond to the news that Darrell has joined the wrestling team?

3. What do you think of Darrell's decision to join the wrestling team? How do you think it will affect his situation at school? List the pros and cons of this decision before coming to your conclusions.

4. Why do you think Amberlynn reacts as she does when Tyray accuses her of liking Darrell? What is your opinion of her reaction?

Chapters 9 and 10

1. What does Jamee tell Darrell when they see each other at the supermarket? Where does she tell him he should go?

2. What happens between Darrell

and Tyray at the school dance? What does Darrell do afterward?

3. What is your opinion of how Darrell responds to Uncle Jason's criticism? What are some other ways Darrell could have responded? Make a list of what you think Darrell's options are in dealing with Uncle Jason.

4. Darrell feels as if wrestling hasn't changed anything for him, since Tyray is still bullying him. Do you agree? Give reasons for your answer.

Chapters 11 and 12

1. What does Darrell discover Travis doing to Nate in the garage? What is Darrell's reaction?

2. What does the principal decide to do with Darrell and Tyray?

3. Do you agree that the principal was right to treat Darrell differently from Tyray following the cafeteria incident? In other words, is the principal's decision fair? Provide reasons for your answers.

4. Pretend you are Darrell at the end of the story. Write a letter admitting to

your mother what you've been going through since you moved to California, focusing on the situation with Tyray. Be sure to explain why you haven't told her the truth sooner about what's been going on.

A Bluford High testimonial from Jim Blasingame, Associate Professor of English, Arizona State University

I am going to unabashedly push the Bluford High Series because I have heard so many testimonies to their success with kids, both struggling readers and those who read at or above grade level. Among the high interest/low reading level offerings available right now, these books are getting rave reviews from teachers and young readers.

Teachers have said that they, themselves, find the books to be interesting reads because the stories are so good. Each book revolves around events that take place at fictitious Bluford High School, somewhere in California. The setting is urban, and the kids face urban sorts of issues, as well as the issues that all teens seem to face at some point, regardless of where they live.

We have published reviews of almost every book in the series in the Books for Adolescents section of IRA's *Journal of Adolescent and Adult Literacy*, including father/daughter paired reviews done by Arizona State University Professor of African American Literature, Dr. Neal Lester, and his daughter, Jasmine, a student at Desert Vista High School here in Phoenix.

Jim Blasingame is president of the Arizona English Teachers' Association. He is the co-editor of The ALAN Review, *and editor of the Books for Adolescents column in* The Journal of Adolescent and Adult Literacy. *He is the author of* Books That Don't Bore 'Em: Young Adult Books that Speak to this Generation *(Scholastic, 2007).*

THE BLUFORD HIGH SERIES

Read them all!

Lost and Found
by Anne Schraff; 0-439-89839-0; $3.99
Darcy Wills is in big trouble. First there was the mysterious stranger who started following her. Then there was the threatening note left on her desk. And now her sister has disappeared. Forced into a desperate race against time, Darcy must take action to save her sister — and her fragile family — before it is too late.

A Matter of Trust
by Anne Schraff; 0-439-86547-6; $3.99
In grade school, Darcy and Brisana were friends. But all that has changed. Now the former friends are bitter rivals, and the tension between them is getting worse. Darcy tries to stay calm, ignoring her old friend's daily taunts. But when she learns that Brisana is after her boyfriend, Hakeem Randall, Darcy knows she must do something.

Secrets in the Shadows
by Anne Schraff; 0-439-90485-4; $3.99
Roylin Bailey is living a nightmare. It started when the new student arrived in his history class. She was the most beautiful girl he had ever seen, and she seemed to like him. But when Roylin tried to impress her, he made a terrible mistake. Caught in a tightening web of lies and threats, Roylin is desperate for a way out.

Someone to Love Me
by Anne Schraff; 0-439-90486-2; $3.99
At first, Bobby Wallace was everything Cindy Gibson hoped for. He was the perfect escape from her problems in school and even bigger troubles at home. But then, Bobby starts behaving strangely, and Cindy soon finds herself in the worst trouble of her life.

The Bully
by Paul Langan; 0-439-86546-8; $3.99
A new school. A new bully. That's what Darrell Mercer faces when he and his mom move from Philadelphia to

California. But Darrell's lived in fear long enough, and now he must decide whether to run—or fight back.

Payback
by Paul Langan; 0-439-90487-0; $3.99
Tyray was one of the most feared students in school—until the kids he once bullied started fighting back.

Until We Meet Again
by Anne Schraff; 0-439-90488-9; $3.99
When bad news threatens to tear Darcy and her boyfriend apart, Darcy must make a decision that will change her life forever.

Blood Is Thicker
by Paul Langan and D.M. Blackwell; 0-439-90489-7; $3.99
Hakeem and his cousin Savon have grown apart, but when circumstances force the cousins to live together, they'll have to find a way to get along.

COMING IN 2008

Brothers in Arms
by Paul Langan and Ben Alirez; 0-439-90490-0; $3.99
Martin Luna is in deep trouble. Just months ago, a horrible tragedy took his little brother, and now it threatens to take him too. Martin now stands at a crossroad, with his life hanging in the balance. Which way will he go?

Summer of Secrets
by Paul Langan; 0-439-90491-9; $3.99
Darcy Wills needs help. A frightening ordeal at the end of the school year has turned her world upside down. Unable to deny the painful truth she's been hiding, Darcy turns to her remaining friends, only to discover one of them has an even bigger secret. Now, Darcy must take a stand for herself — and for her friend.

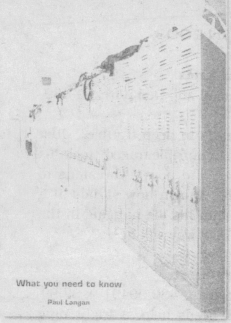